"Dinah Halstead?"

"I'm Charlotte. I'm Dinah's identical twin sister," she said. "But those criminals think I'm Dinah. I don't know what's going on."

He heard the voice of the unknown assailant; it was clear he was angry. And it sounded like he was headed their direction.

"My truck's parked near the alley where I first saw you. Come on, let's get out of here." He held out his hand, praying she would reach for it and let him take her to safety. After a moment's hesitation, Charlotte grasped it. They took off running. Wade slowed his pace as they approached his truck.

"What?" she asked in alarm.

"I just want to make sure everything's okay." If he were one of the bad guys, he'd be waiting here for the bounty hunter to return.

Overhead the clouds were moving, and in the subtle glow of moonlight he saw a large puddle behind his truck, the standing water's surface perfectly smooth.

But then it rippled. For no discernible reason.

"Back up!" Wade ordered.

"But why? I thought—"

Bang!

Jenna Night comes from a family of Southern-born natural storytellers. Her parents were avid readers and the house was always filled with books. No wonder she grew up wanting to tell her own stories. She's lived on both coasts but currently resides in the Inland Northwest, where she's astonished by the occasional glimpse of a moose, a herd of elk or a soaring eagle.

Books by Jenna Night

Love Inspired Suspense

Range River Bounty Hunters

Abduction in the Dark
Fugitive Ambush
Mistaken Twin Target

Rock Solid Bounty Hunters

Fugitive Chase
Hostage Pursuit
Cold Case Manhunt

Last Stand Ranch
High Desert Hideaway
Killer Country Reunion
Justice at Morgan Mesa
Lost Rodeo Memories
Colorado Manhunt
"Twin Pursuit"

Visit the Author Profile page at LoveInspired.com.

MISTAKEN TWIN TARGET

JENNA NIGHT

LOVE INSPIRED SUSPENSE
INSPIRATIONAL ROMANCE

LOVE INSPIRED® SUSPENSE
INSPIRATIONAL ROMANCE

ISBN-13: 978-1-335-58754-1

Mistaken Twin Target

Recycling programs
for this product may
not exist in your area.

Love Inspired
22 Adelaide St. West, 41st Floor
Toronto, Ontario M5H 4E3, Canada
www.LoveInspired.com

Printed in U.S.A.

Let not mercy and truth forsake thee: bind them about thy neck; write them upon the table of thine heart.
—*Proverbs* 3:3

To my mom, Esther.

ONE

Charlotte Halstead hurried down the dark street, anxious to reach her SUV and get out of the wind and rain rolling through Range River, Idaho.

Her dinner meeting at a steak house with a literacy advocacy group had run late and she was the only member at the gathering who'd parked in the municipal lot a couple of blocks away. The street was nearly empty, and as she passed by a jewelry store and then a real-estate office, both shuttered up for the night, a nervous itch crawled up her spine.

She slowed down and threw a quick glance over her shoulder. Of course no one was following her. "Get a grip," she muttered to herself as she resumed her quick pace. "You're in Range River, not Seattle." She'd been back in her hometown for six weeks, focused on work and defying her mother's push to pursue a romantic life because pouring her heart into a cold, businesslike relationship like her parents had and calling it a *marriage* was the last thing she wanted. She took a breath to calm her squirmy nerves. Apparently it was going to take her a little longer to readjust to safer, small-town living.

A band of heavier rain swept up the street toward

her; she could see it coming in the amber glow from the streetlights, and she pulled the hood of her jacket farther down over her face.

Finally, she reached the parking lot. She approached her SUV, hit the key fob to unlock it and then quickly slid into the driver's seat, pulling the door shut beside her.

Safe and sound. Nothing to worry about. She tossed her tote onto the seat beside her, pulled back her hood and turned to the rearview mirror to fix what she was certain would be an unruly head of hair.

A stranger sat behind her.

Inside her SUV.

Charlotte's body startled at the shock of it.

Her lungs locked up and she couldn't scream, couldn't even take a breath. Fear washed over her like a giant wave, leaving her light-headed and numb. She fumbled for the door handle, desperate to obey the internal voice screaming, *Get out now!*

The intruder catapulted himself forward from the very back of the SUV to the second row. In an instant he was just inches behind her. He scooted even closer and slung an arm and shoulder over her seat back so he could press a gun to her temple.

She was finally able to scream, but it did her no good.

Too late, she realized that the phone alert from her car alarm an hour ago had not been the random, nuisance triggering she had assumed it to be when she'd hit reset and continued with her meeting. Because of that mistake, her life now hung by a thread.

Oh, Lord. Help!

A surge of adrenaline and fear sent her body shaking.

"Don't make a move unless I tell you to." The intruder's voice was low and gravelly and she caught a whiff of stale cigarette smoke on his breath. "You try to get away, try to make noise to get people's attention, and I'll kill you. Believe me. I don't care whether you live or die."

The oddly emotionless tone of his voice made him all the more believable.

"What do you want?" Charlotte's words came out breathy and puffy now that her lungs had loosened and she was gulping in air. Her heart galloped in her chest and a matching pulse pounded in her ears.

"My bag is right there." She started to gesture toward her tote, but caught herself at the last moment when she realized that any movement might give him an excuse to pull the trigger. "It's in the seat next to me," she finally added. "Go ahead, take my wallet. Take whatever you want. I'll get out and you can have the SUV."

"I'll take what I want later."

Later? Why not now?

Charlotte turned her gaze to the rearview mirror. The intruder was staring back at her reflection. "Don't look at me," he barked. "Face straight ahead."

Charlotte forced her gaze back to the redbrick exterior of the building in front of her.

"Start the engine." The thug moved so that he sat directly behind Charlotte, and he tilted his gun so the barrel tip pressed against the back of her head. "I'll be watching everything you do. If you flash your headlights at an oncoming car to get the driver's attention, or blow through a stop sign, or drive too fast hoping a cop will pull you over, I will shoot you. I'm getting paid to deliver you to a specific location. Nobody said you had to be alive when you got there."

Somebody was paying him to kidnap her? Who would do that? Why?

Charlotte started the engine. "Where are we going?" She was still terrified, in some ways more so, but the light-headedness had eased and her mind was starting to clear. She needed to focus her thoughts and watch for any opportunity to save herself.

"Never mind where we're going. You just do what I tell you. Start by driving out of the parking lot and turning left."

Charlotte's knees shook as she alternately tapped the brakes and the gas pedal to back out of the parking slot and get to the street. She hesitated at the edge of the driveway when it came time to make the left turn. A right turn would take her toward the police department, although it was several miles and many more turns away. If she tried to go in that direction, the kidnapper would kill her.

It was eight o'clock on a Wednesday night in early March, so there wasn't much traffic. No one drove by for her to signal in hopes of getting help. The winter tourists were gone and the summer tourists hadn't arrived yet. Cold, rainy early spring wasn't much of a draw for the North Idaho mountain town.

The abductor shoved his gun harder against her head. "Get out of this parking lot and onto the street, *now!*"

Charlotte hit the gas and made the turn onto the street. She fought to take a deep breath as a rising surge of panic threatened to choke her. Range River was a moderate-size town surrounded by forest. If the thug made her drive past the edge of town, into the forest, what then? Nothing good, obviously. Beyond that, she didn't want to imagine.

Driving as slowly as she dared, Charlotte desperately tried to think of a way to escape without getting herself shot. But with that gun pointed at her, anything she did could get her killed in an instant.

A few moments passed and then she heard the criminal make a phone call while still managing to keep his gun pressed against Charlotte's head.

She could just barely hear the call go through and someone answer at the other end.

"I got Dinah," the abductor said. "We're on our way now."

Dinah?

"You've got the wrong person!" Charlotte called out. He'd let her go now, wouldn't he? "I'm not Dinah," she continued. "I'm Charlotte."

The person on the other end of the call must have heard her, because the man in the car said, "She's lying. She's Dinah Halstead. I've got the picture of Dinah you sent right here on my phone. This is her." A moment later he added, "Right." And then the call ended.

"No, seriously, you've made a mistake. Dinah is my sister. My identical twin sister." Charlotte felt a stab of guilt as the words poured out of her. But she wasn't shoving her sister under the bus, putting her in danger. She just wanted the creep to let her go. Then she could get to the police, report what had happened, and they would make sure Dinah was protected while the cops got this bizarre situation figured out.

"Identical twin sister? Give me a break." The gunman made a scoffing sound.

"No, wait," Charlotte said, fanning a spark of hope in the midst of the horrible situation. "If you would just search on your phone—"

"Shut up!" This time he shoved the gun hard to make her head snap forward.

"Okay, *okay.*" She gripped the steering wheel tighter, fighting against her frustration. If she could stay calm, maybe she could get him to listen to her.

"Turn left," he barked as they approached the next intersection.

"Why do you want Dinah?" she asked while making the turn.

Several moments passed, but he didn't respond.

"I'm not Dinah!" Charlotte finally shouted.

So much for trying to appear calm. But the situation was absurd. "*Look* in my purse, *look* at my driver's license. You'll see my true identity."

"You just want to distract me so you can try to get away."

Charlotte huffed out a breath, a tight feeling of anger starting to overtake the grip of fear. "Why won't you just take a look?"

"Shut up." He didn't bother yelling this time. He just let the words ooze out, filled with contempt.

What would he and his accomplice do when they discovered he'd grabbed the wrong woman? Kill her so she couldn't turn them in to the cops? She wanted to believe they'd let her go, but it didn't seem likely.

But she wouldn't give up. She *couldn't.*

Charlotte leaned toward the passenger seat to grab her tote. "Look, let me just grab my wallet and you can see—"

"Enough!" The man grabbed a handful of her hair, twisted it and yanked her head back until it smacked into the headrest. "I don't *care.*"

"Okay," Charlotte said quickly.

He ordered her to make several more turns until they were in an industrial part of town.

"Slow down. Turn into the alley."

Fear turned into dread. A dark, heavy sensation sank into her chest. The kidnapper still pressed his gun to her head, still held on to a fistful of her hair. She made the turn into the alley. She had no choice.

She drove a short distance into the shadowy passage until he told her to stop.

She had to *do* something. She just needed a chance.

Charlotte hit the brakes and her SUV came to a stop. Her body tensed. Maybe he was going to shoot her right here.

Dear Lord, protect me.

He let go of her hair and took the tip of his gun away from her head. He moved to open the car door.

Charlotte yanked on her own door handle and was out of the SUV in an instant, pure terror fueling her as she ran down the dark alley in the cold, heavy rain.

Just to the end of the alley, she told herself. *And then to the cross street where there might be somebody driving by and you can get help.* A few of the businesses were still staffed and functioning even at this late hour. Maybe she could flag down a worker and get them to call the police.

She was closing in on her goal when headlights swept around the corner of a warehouse and headed up the alley straight for her. The approaching vehicle slammed to a halt, the door flung open and the driver stepped out.

Charlotte could barely see his outline in the darkness, but she kept running. She couldn't turn around and run back toward the kidnapper. She dared to hope this new arrival would offer her help.

That hope was quickly dashed when her abductor— hot on her heels—shouted, *"Get her!"*

The driver stepped into the illumination cast by the car's headlights and pointed a gun at Charlotte. She came to a halt. Disappointment and hopelessness smacked her with a force that nearly knocked her to her knees. So much for her attempt at escape. She'd just run from one dangerous criminal to another.

Bounty hunter Wade Fast Horse hit the brakes, pulled over to the side of the narrow road and brought his pickup truck to a stop. Ahead, red taillights reflected on rain-slicked asphalt at the end of an alley.

He was following bail jumper Brett Gamble, a fugitive who'd recently been arrested for residential burglary. The guy only had a couple of assault charges on his record, none of them involving weapons, so Wade figured he could capture him on his own rather than having someone from his team accompany him.

A warrant had been issued for Gamble after he'd skipped his court appearance earlier in the day. Range River Bail Bonds had bonded Gamble out of jail, so it was now Wade's job to find the bail violator and haul him back to county lockup. Wade had spotted Gamble a short time ago inside a Thai restaurant where the fugitive's girlfriend worked, but he hadn't arrested him on the spot because there were families with children around. Following the fugitive home and arresting him there seemed like a better choice.

But Gamble had not headed home after finishing his dinner. Instead, he'd driven to a section of town with warehouses and a few small factories where he'd just now turned down an alley and then stopped.

Had his fugitive figured out he was being followed? Was he trying to hide in the alley or was something else going on? It was possible that Gamble was more of a threat than his criminal record indicated. People committed crimes they were never charged for all the time. Maybe he'd done something dangerous that Wade didn't know about.

Wade grabbed his baseball cap from the seat beside him, hoping it would keep some of the rain out of his eyes, and then got out of the truck to see what his bail jumper was up to. The guy had been arrested for burglary, so maybe he was here to sell stolen items to someone.

Wade jogged over to a warehouse, pressed against a wall to stay hidden and then peered around the corner into the alley. What he saw wasn't anything he'd anticipated.

A woman stood in front of Gamble's car, frozen in place, while Gamble and a second man Wade had never seen before pointed guns at her.

Clearly the situation had the potential for explosive violence. Wade needed to call the cops. Bounty hunters were not law enforcement officers and there were strict limits on what they could do. At the same time, like any Good Samaritan, he was within his rights to help a person in harm's way.

Keeping his gaze locked on the trio in front of him, Wade reached for his phone. Just as his fingers touched it, Gamble suddenly moved toward the woman in an agitated fashion, gun pointed at her, saying something that Wade couldn't clearly hear. It looked like he was about to shoot.

"Freeze!" Wade stepped around the corner of the warehouse, going for his gun instead of his phone. "Drop your weapons!"

The fugitive spun around. Wade had the advantage of being in darkness. He hoped the bad guys would assume he was a cop. That they'd think they were surrounded and put down their guns.

Instead, the unidentified man fired several shots in Wade's direction, forcing the bounty hunter to retreat and go back to peering around the corner of the warehouse. Gamble ducked out of the way. The woman took off running up the alley and then darted into a passage between two buildings.

Gamble sprang up and ran after her.

Wade was determined to get to her first.

Instead of running down the alley behind them, he raced along the narrow, intersecting road, hoping to get ahead of them and reach the woman before Gamble caught up with her.

He raced past alleys and narrow service roads, looking down each one as he went by, hoping to see either his fugitive or the woman. He didn't see either one. Somehow, they'd gotten ahead of him. Or they'd turned down a connecting passage and gone off in an unknown direction where he'd never find them in time.

The smartest thing for him to do was to stop and *listen* for some indication of which way they'd gone. He stepped into one of the alleys, where sound bounced off the walls and carried a little better, hoping to hear footfalls or voices or trash cans being knocked over. Something, *anything*, that would give him an idea of their location.

For several seconds, the only thing he heard was rain splattering on the asphalt around him. And then, *footsteps*. Fast slapping and splashing sounds moved through a passage toward him.

The bounty hunter pressed against the side of a building, doing his best to make himself invisible in the darkness. Seconds later, the unidentified man ran into view. He had a phone in his hand, set to speaker. He stopped and spoke into it, coordinating with Gamble to locate the woman they were chasing. Looking up and down the alley, cursing, the man raked the fingers of his free hand through his hair.

Wade didn't move. Much as he wanted to tackle and handcuff the guy, it wouldn't keep the woman from danger since Gamble was still searching for her. But if he followed the thug, the assailant might lead Wade right to her.

The unidentified man started moving again, jogging up the alley before disappearing into another passage between buildings.

Wade started up the alley behind him, but after taking several steps he caught a flash of movement from the corner of his eye.

He slowed and turned for a closer look.

The woman sprang up from behind a stack of pallets and smacked Wade on the side of the head with a chunk of asphalt she must have grabbed from the crumbling edge of the alley.

Wincing in pain, he grabbed her wrists before she could do any further damage. "Shh!" he whispered as she opened her mouth to scream. "They'll hear you and find you."

By the faint illumination cast by a lone security light farther down the alley, he saw the cornered-animal look of sheer terror in her eyes. She dropped the chunk of asphalt. And then she kicked him, the pointy toe of her boot connecting hard with his shin. Again, he winced.

But he didn't loosen his grip. "I'm trying to help you!" he said through gritted teeth, shaking her wrists, hoping to break the grip of panic that was understandably overwhelming her. "I'm a bounty hunter. I'm tracking Brett Gamble and I saw what happened. I saw him pointing a gun at you."

She stared at him as if he made no sense.

In that moment, he realized she looked familiar. "Dinah Halstead?" What was the daughter of the owners of the luxury Wolf Lake Resort doing in an alley at night with a couple of criminals?

She was probably just one more spoiled, rich young woman foolishly looking for excitement in the wrong place. Wade crossed paths with her type every now and then while in pursuit of a fugitive. There was no way he would put up with anyone like that in his personal life.

"I'm *Charlotte*. I am *not* Dinah," the woman snapped. Wade was pretty sure those were tears of frustration and not raindrops building up in the corners of her eyes.

"I'm Dinah's identical twin sister," she continued. "But those men think I'm Dinah." She tried to pull her wrists free and Wade released his grip. She rubbed her eyes. "I don't know what's going on."

The rain had slackened and then stopped, and in the relative quiet he heard the voice of the unknown assailant. He couldn't discern the man's words, but it was clear he was angry. And it sounded like he was headed back in their direction.

"My truck's parked near the alley where I first saw you. Come on—let's get out of here." He held out his hand, praying that she would reach for it and let him take her to safety.

He did have a gun. And if he had to, he could use it

to defend the both of them. But he wanted to avoid a shoot-out if at all possible. Once people started firing, and bullets ricocheted off buildings and asphalt, there was no controlling where the rounds would go. Innocent people could get hurt.

After a moment's hesitation, Charlotte grasped his hand.

They took off running, to the end of the alley and then down the intersecting street toward Wade's truck. Gamble's vehicle had vanished but Charlotte's SUV was still there.

Wade slowed his pace as they approached his truck. He stepped in front of Charlotte and stopped.

"What?" she asked in alarm.

"I just want to make sure everything's okay." There weren't any other passenger vehicles parked nearby, so it would have been obvious to the bad guys that this truck belonged to Wade. If he were one of the bad guys, he'd be waiting here for the bounty hunter to return.

Overhead the clouds were moving, and in the subtle glow of moonlight he saw a large puddle behind his truck, the standing water's surface perfectly smooth.

But then it rippled. For no discernible reason.

Maybe someone was crouched back there.

"Back up!" Wade ordered.

"But why? I thought—"

Wade stepped back, grabbed Charlotte's hand, and they ran toward the nearest building. It was some type of factory, closed for the night, with trucks and large storage containers parked in the lot that surrounded it.

Bang!

A shot blasted toward them from the direction of Wade's truck.

Bang! Bang!

Wade tightened his grip on Charlotte's hand and he pulled her in front of him. A few steps later he gave her a slight shove, sending her between two semis with large shipping containers that were backed up and parked at a loading dock. He gave her a boost when they reached the concrete dock and then jumped up alongside her. They scooted over until they were hidden between the end of a shipping container and the loading dock roll-up door.

"Call the police," Wade whispered as he reached for his gun. If the assailants came upon them, he'd do what he had to do.

"I don't have my phone."

Wade handed her his.

She tapped the screen, and moments later she whispered into it, giving their location and explaining what had happened.

At the same time, Wade heard Gamble and the other assailant talking to one another as they converged near the truck where Wade and Charlotte were hiding.

"The cops have already gotten reports of shots fired out here and they're on their way," Charlotte whispered to Wade.

Thank You, Lord.

She had the volume turned down and the phone to her ear, but Wade could still hear the emergency operator talking to her.

The bad guys were getting closer and Wade was concerned that the sounds from the phone would carry and give away their location.

"We need to silence my phone," he whispered, taking it from her and tapping the appropriate side buttons.

The assailants' voices grew louder as they moved

closer. Charlotte pressed against Wade's side. He felt her shiver in the cold, damp darkness.

A rectangle of light illuminated the area near where they were hiding. A second, similar type of light joined it.

"They're using the flashlights from their phones to search for us," Charlotte whispered into his ear.

Wade took a steadying breath, watching the lights move closer.

The men didn't bother to move quietly. But after a few moments, Wade heard something different.

Sirens. In the distance and rapidly drawing closer.

Charlotte squeezed his arm. "Police." She whispered the word barely louder than a breath.

Both searchlights suddenly went out. The bad guys must have heard the sirens, too. "You owe me, Dinah!" Gamble yelled. "And you're not going to get out of paying! I'll make sure of it." The threat was followed by the fading sound of rapid footsteps as the assailants fled.

Moments later, blue police lights flashed across the storage containers and the loading dock.

Charlotte scrambled to her feet. "I need to tell them my sister's in danger."

Wade helped her climb down from the dock and watched her run to the first arriving patrol car. He had no idea what the bigger story was here. Clearly, Dinah Halstead was the person the goons were after. But he couldn't help thinking that Charlotte might still be in danger, too.

TWO

An hour later, Charlotte was at the police station. Officers had retrieved her SUV and checked it for potential prints left by the kidnapper. Her tote and phone had just been returned to her and she finally had the opportunity to call her sister to tell her what had happened and warn her that she was in danger.

Dinah had reacted with shock and disbelief.

"I don't owe anybody anything," Dinah responded emphatically after Charlotte told her about the assailant's threat. "The creep who says I do is delusional. Or he's the latest opportunist trying to get some of our family money."

"Well, he believes what he said, so you need to be careful. Don't go anywhere alone. Not until these men are caught. Where are you right now?"

"I'm at the resort. I was in the Garnet Banquet Room, but I stepped into the lobby to take your call. The Bellinghem Property Managers Association awards ceremony is still going on. Ethan is here, as well. He wanted us to stand by in case there are any problems. You know how he is."

Ethan Frey, Dinah's boyfriend, had started his career at Wolf Lake Resort working as a parking lot attendant when he was a teenager. He worked his way up over the years, leaving town to earn a couple of degrees, and then returning to eventually become the resort's chief operations officer. He was older than Dinah, steadier, and had a stronger work ethic. The two of them had started dating a year ago.

"Enough worrying about me," Dinah continued. "How are *you*? Shouldn't you go to the hospital to get checked for injuries?"

"I'm fine." Charlotte glanced around the police station conference room where she'd been sent to wait. She'd been given a blanket to wrap around her rain-soaked shoulders when she'd first arrived, along with a cup of strong, hot coffee. The bounty hunter who'd helped her escape the kidnappers—she'd learned his name was Wade Fast Horse—also sat in the conference room. Unlike her, he'd declined the offer of a blanket and he didn't appear particularly put out by having to sit at the oval conference table in soaking wet clothes. Maybe as a *bounty hunter* he spent a lot of time tracking people in the rain. Who knew what bounty hunters did?

"Charlotte!"

Charlotte moved the phone slightly away from her ear. "What? Why are you yelling?"

"I just asked if you wanted Ethan and I to come get you and you didn't answer."

"Oh." Charlotte shook her head and tried to redirect her thoughts. Now that things had calmed down, and she knew Dinah was safe, her body had started trembling again and her mind wouldn't stay focused. She recognized what was happening as an adrenaline crash and drew in a deep, fortifying breath, intent on holding herself together. "Thanks, but I'll ask an officer to drive me home." After all she'd been through, driving herself didn't seem like such a good idea right now. "I can retrieve my SUV later," she added.

"Have you spoken to Mom and Dad about this?" Dinah asked.

"Not yet. And don't you tell them, either. I want to wait until they can see me in person and know I'm okay."

"You don't sound okay," Dinah muttered.

Truth was Charlotte didn't feel okay. Not emotionally, anyway. She'd nearly gotten killed tonight, and the reality of that was hitting her hard, making her exhausted and jittery at the same time. "I should go. The detective will be here any minute. I guess she'll ask me a few more questions and then I can go home."

"I'm so sorry this happened to you." Dinah went from sounding like Charlotte's bold, confident younger sister— by sixteen minutes—to sounding fearful and worried, which was *not* like Dinah. And then it sounded like she'd started crying. "I'll see you when you get here."

They disconnected and Charlotte tossed her phone into her tote. She pulled the blanket tighter around her shoulders. Her gaze settled on the bounty hunter. "Thank you for saving my life." After the cops arrived at the crime scene, she hadn't had an opportunity to talk to the man who'd come to her rescue. Until now, the police had been intent on interviewing them separately.

He'd been politely averting his gaze since she initiated her call to Dinah. Now he turned to her. His deep brown eyes appeared hardened and determined, his expression angry. But then he blinked, offered her a faint smile, and his gaze brimmed with warmth and compassion. "Glad I could help."

Charlotte was taken aback by the sudden change.

She'd heard about bounty hunters, seen them in movies and on TV shows, and had the impression that they were rough, tough and hardheaded. She'd experienced what it was like to have this particular bounty hunter by her side in real life amid some terrifying moments. He'd been relatively calm and decisive. And while he hadn't exactly seemed *comfortable* with danger, he appeared to be used to it.

Now that they were in the conference room together, she was getting her first good look at him in decent lighting. Black hair, aquiline features, nearly black eyes, reddish-brown skin. A few seconds ago he'd looked fierce, but now the smile he offered bordered on shy.

Charlotte cleared her throat, remembering how she'd pressed against him for reassurance as they sat on the loading dock listening to the thugs closing in on them.

Turning to someone for emotional reassurance like that was unusual for her. Her childhood had been spent with distracted parents and resort employees who only pretended to care about her because that was their job. She'd learned early that depending on someone to shore her up emotionally only led to heartbreak and bitter disappointment.

Hence her determination to focus on work rather than looking for a husband, despite her mother's ambitions for her. Charlotte would rather be single than be married and risk feeling the hollow pain of living with another person nearby yet still feeling alone. Yes, she felt a little lonesome sometimes, but she was not interested in building a life together with anyone. The truth was she could only safely rely on herself.

Even so, the admittedly handsome bounty hunter

had shown up at just the right time to keep her from getting killed, and she appreciated it. She searched for something else to say to keep the conversation going, because despite her intention to remain aloof, she was curious about him. They'd crossed paths at a profoundly significant moment in her life and she wanted to know something more about him beyond just his profession and his name.

But before she could say anything, the door to the conference room opened and Detective Romanov, the auburn-haired investigator Charlotte had spoken with briefly before being ushered into the conference room, walked in. Wade got to his feet and waited until the detective was seated before he sat down again.

Charlotte couldn't help being impressed by his good manners.

Romanov looked at an electronic tablet for a few moments and then set it aside. She glanced at Wade and then Charlotte before settling her focus back on Wade. "Tell me how you and Ms. Halstead know each other."

"What?" Charlotte piped up before the bounty hunter could answer. "We don't know each other at all."

Romanov lifted an eyebrow, still gazing at Wade. "So you decided to jump in and risk your life for a complete stranger? She's not a client? Or connected to one of your clients?"

He offered a slight shrug. "Like I said in my initial statement, I was hunting Brett Gamble after his bond had been revoked when I came across him and another man I'd never seen before holding Ms. Halstead at gunpoint. It looked to me like Gamble was about to take a shot at her. I had to do something."

Romanov turned to Charlotte. "So, how are you, Mr.

Gamble and our currently unidentified assailant connected? I need to know the truth no matter how ugly it might be."

"I honestly have never seen either of the men before in my life."

"In your statement you mentioned Gamble claiming that your sister owed him money for some reason. What do you think that was about?"

Charlotte shook her head. "I have no idea."

"Gamble was recently arrested for residential burglary. None of the stolen items, including several pieces of high-dollar jewelry, have been recovered. Might your sister have agreed to purchase something from him at a suspiciously reduced price? And then perhaps she didn't pay him?"

"Why would she do that?" Charlotte was starting to feel defensive.

The detective kept her cool gaze fixed on Charlotte but didn't respond to her question.

"No," Charlotte finally said. "I don't think she bought stolen goods."

"Gamble also has a history of violence," the detective continued. "Could your sister have hired him to threaten somebody? Maybe she needed him to frighten someone into ending some kind of dispute and she didn't pay him for his services?"

Charlotte stared wordlessly at her. What a bizarre string of accusations. "Dinah's n-not like that," she finally stammered. "She works at the resort, just like I do. I work in Marketing. Our parents assigned her the coffee shop on the plaza to manage and she's been doing a good job." Despite the fervor of her words, a shadowy uncertainty flickered through Charlotte's mind. She would know if things weren't going well for her sister, wouldn't she?

Charlotte and Dinah had gone their separate ways after high school, with Dinah attending their mother's alma mater on the East Coast while Charlotte headed for Seattle. A couple of internships plus some added courses had kept Charlotte away for an extra year. The sisters, women of very different temperaments, hadn't been emotionally close to one another for the last five years, despite being twins.

Charlotte had only been back in Range River for six weeks. Even so, if something odd had been going on with Dinah, wouldn't she have noticed?

Charlotte tried to shake off the feeling of uncertainty about her sister, but it stubbornly stayed in her mind. Detective Romanov had to entertain every plausible idea that crossed her mind in order to solve this crime. That didn't mean any of her far-fetched theories were true. She drew in a breath and lifted her chin. "Detective, I want to do everything I can to help you. I want the criminals who tried to kill me—*us*—" she quickly glanced at Wade "—to be captured and locked up. But I will *not* drag my sister's reputation through the mud. She is in *danger*, and I think your line of questioning borders on blaming the victim in this situation."

Romanov gave a slight nod. "A lot of people make bad decisions that get them into serious trouble," the detective said mildly. "Then they ask the police for help, as they should, but they withhold important details and that puts them in greater danger. I want to make sure that doesn't happen here."

While she understood the detective's point of view, Charlotte still couldn't help feeling insulted on behalf of her sister. She crossed her arms over her chest. "Why aren't you out looking for Brett Gamble and his lowlife partner?"

"Officers are searching for Gamble at his home and elsewhere as we speak. I'll have a lineup of mug shots for you to look at tomorrow and hopefully we'll get a name for the unidentified assailant. As soon as businesses reopen in the morning, we'll collect all available security video near the location where you were initially abducted and also in the industrial district where you met Mr. Fast Horse. This investigation has not ground to a halt just because I'm sitting here talking with you."

That sounded reasonable. Charlotte nodded. "Thank you."

"You'll need to come back and have a look at the mug shots, too," Romanov said to Wade.

"Just let me know what time."

Romanov picked up her tablet and got to her feet. "All right, Charlotte. Let's get you home. I understand you live on the resort property?"

"That's right." Charlotte rose, took the blanket from her shoulders, folded it and set it on a chair.

"Does Dinah live on the resort property, as well?" the detective asked.

"Yes."

"Good. I want to talk to her. Tonight."

Wade stood. "I'd like to come along."

"Why?" Charlotte turned to him, uncertain how a bounty hunter could figure into a kidnapping and attempted murder investigation.

"Brett Gamble is still a bail jumper and I'm still going after him," Wade answered, shifting his gaze between Charlotte and the detective. "Your sister might have useful information about him without realizing it. Maybe when she sees his mug shot she'll realize she's seen him somewhere or that she knows him by another name. That information could help me find him."

Romanov gave a nod that seemed to indicate her approval of his request before walking out of the conference room.

Charlotte followed the detective, realizing as she did so that her knees had gotten wobbly again. She'd survived tonight's attack, but the memories of having a gun pressed to her head and running for her life down a dark alley rattled her to her core. Even more unnerving was the fact that the assailants were still at large. They were free to launch another attack on Charlotte—or her twin sister—at any time.

Detective Romanov, accompanied by a uniformed police officer, drove Charlotte to the Wolf Lake Resort. Wade followed in his truck. When they stepped into the marble-floored lobby, Charlotte's twin hurried forward to embrace her.

Dinah Halstead wore her blond hair tightly pulled back, twisted and pinned up. Her makeup was perfectly applied to dramatic effect. She wore black trousers and a gold sweater with a little bit of sparkle. She was a beautiful woman, no doubt, but Wade's gaze was drawn back to Charlotte. He found her casual appearance—jeans, flannel shirt and jacket—and the warm, open expression in her eyes more appealing.

Not that anybody asked him.

Dinah's boyfriend, Ethan, had come to the lobby alongside her. He sported a suit and tie and appeared to be a decade older than the Halstead twins.

The sisters held each other in a tight embrace for several moments. Charlotte managed to keep her composure, but Dinah burst into tears. After they let go of each other, introductions were made.

"A bounty hunter?" Dinah said to Wade when his turn came. "What do we need a bounty hunter for?"

"One of the attackers was a bail jumper," Wade answered easily. "It's my job to find him."

"I'd like to speak with you for a few minutes," Detective Romanov said to Dinah, redirecting the topic back to her investigation. "One of the assailants mentioned you by name."

"Yes, of course." Dinah wiped at her eyes. "Charlotte told me about that."

"Why don't we head up to your parents' apartment," Ethan suggested to Dinah after glancing toward several resort employees at the check-in desk who were casting curious looks in their direction.

The small group walked around a corner and through a door leading to a private elevator. Romanov and the officer followed close behind Dinah and Ethan. Wade brought up the rear. He was surprised when Charlotte dropped back to walk with him. "Our parents have an apartment on the top floor as well as a house on the edge of the resort property near the lake," she said.

"I know."

"You do?" Charlotte sounded surprised.

"My mother worked here when I was a little kid."

"Oh really?" She offered him a slight smile. "Which department?"

"Housekeeping," he answered as everyone stepped into the elevator. "She cleaned up after rich people who were on vacation." The sharpness in his tone took Wade

by surprise. A cluster of memories and emotions were
stirred up as the elevator took them to the top floor.
There was nothing wrong with the work his mom did
back in the days after his dad left them. And Maribel
Fast Horse never complained about it. But she came
home from work every night bone-tired. At some point
Wade had started to feel like she was unappreciated,
and that had bothered him.

Later, she'd joined forces with friend and neighbor
Connor Ryan when he opened Range River Bail Bonds.
Life had gotten much better for Wade and his mom after
that. Connor and the other members of the Ryan family
made it obvious that they were grateful for his mom's
work as an investigator, a researcher and an adminis-
trator. He'd half forgotten how rough things had been
in the early days. Until now.

Charlotte was admittedly an attractive and intriguing
woman, but she represented a wide gap between people
born into an easy life and those, like his mom and his
friends, who had to work hard for everything they had.
The thought brought with it a sting of recognition that
the attraction he felt toward Charlotte was a betrayal to
everyone he cared about. He needed to put a stop to it.

The elevator doors opened onto a short hallway with
a single door to the right and another to the left. The
door on the right opened and a woman who appeared
to be in her early fifties, shorter and rounder than the
Halstead twins but with the same blond, blue-eyed coloring, stepped out and made a beeline toward Charlotte,
grabbing her in a tight hug. A man hovered close behind her. His features somewhat favored the twins, and
he was tall, which must have given them their height.

Charlotte's mother finally let go of her daughter only

to hold her at arm's length and scan her up and down. "Are you *sure* you're all right?"

"I'm okay, Mom. Really."

On the way into the apartment, Charlotte's father hugged her.

Introductions were made as the visitors were seated on chairs and one of the thickly padded leather sofas. Floor-to-ceiling windows covered one side of the room, with points of light from houses and businesses down below visible in the darkness.

"Perhaps we need our attorney present," Arthur Halstead commented as Detective Romanov pulled her tablet out of its case and prepared to question Dinah.

Dinah shook her head. "I don't need a lawyer."

Beside her, Ethan reached for her hand.

"It might be better if we speak privately," the detective suggested.

Dinah squared her shoulders. "I have nothing to hide."

"Our daughter had some problems with drugs and alcohol while she was in college," Kandace Halstead said calmly. "We know about it, and it's all behind her. We love her and there's nothing she needs to keep secret from us."

Wade watched as Charlotte's brows lifted and her eyes widened. Was she surprised to hear about Dinah's problems in college, or was she surprised that her parents knew about them? And more importantly—as far as Wade was concerned—were these past problems related to what had happened tonight?

"Could the kidnapping and threat be connected to drugs?" Romanov asked, despite the claims that Dinah had left that issue in her past. "Do you owe a drug dealer money?"

"No." Dinah shook her head. "Absolutely not."

"Are you involved in anything else that puts you in contact with criminals in town?"

"No."

Wade wasn't completely convinced by Dinah's protestations. It was fairly apparent that Romanov wasn't, either. Most likely she would find a way, on another day, to ask Dinah those same questions again in private.

"Why do you think someone would attempt to kidnap you and then claim you owed them money?"

"I don't know." Dinah sighed heavily. "I create a lot of content for my social media accounts, trying to influence people to come visit Range River and stay at the resort. We've had a few celebrities stay with us recently, which I've posted about, and that has led to me having a good number of followers. I sometimes get disturbing messages from people who apparently feel we have a personal relationship because they follow my accounts." She grimaced and an expression of disgust crossed her face. "Maybe the attempt to kidnap me tonight is related to that." She shrugged. "That's just a guess."

"How do you know Brett Gamble?" Wade interjected.

Dinah turned to him. "I don't know anyone by that name."

"Someone remind me why we have a bounty hunter in our home," Kandace said in a frosty voice as she stared at Wade.

"Mom, he saved my life," Charlotte said. Her arms were crossed over her stomach and she looked anxious and exhausted.

Romanov tapped her device and handed it to Dinah.

"This is Brett Gamble's booking photo. Does he look familiar?"

Dinah gazed at the picture. "I've never seen this man before."

Ethan leaned closer to her and peered down at the photo. "I don't recognize him, either."

After looking at the image, the Halstead parents gave a similar response.

"It's getting late and my daughters are tired," Arthur said to the detective after returning Romanov's tablet to her. "I think we should wrap this up for the time being so they can get some rest and continue your questioning tomorrow, if necessary."

"Actually, that's all I have to ask for now." Romanov and the officer got to their feet.

As the Halstead parents were seeing everyone to the door, Wade overheard Kandace ask Charlotte, "Do you want to stay here with Dad and I tonight? Or across the hall with Dinah?"

"Thanks, but I want to sleep in my own bed." Fatigue weighted Charlotte's response. "I feel like pulling the blankets over my head and hiding there for a week."

"I'll stay with you at your place." Dinah's tone made it less an offer and more a statement of fact. "So you don't have to be alone."

Their mother nodded her approval. "I'll tell Randall to have the security team keep a close eye on your condo tonight."

"Condo?" Wade asked Charlotte after she and her sister had hugged their parents good-night and the visitors were heading for the elevator. "You don't live here in the main building?"

It wasn't his business where she lived, and she was

going to have resort security keeping an eye on her, anyway, but he still couldn't help worrying. Even if the creeps who'd kidnapped her had finally figured out she wasn't Dinah, they might still come after her. As long as the motivation for the kidnapping remained unclear, anything seemed possible.

"We have a few condos on the resort property that we rent out, and I live in one of them," Charlotte explained. "They're away from the main buildings, closer to the lake."

"I'm familiar with them," he said.

The head of the security team met them in the lobby. While Ethan and Dinah spoke with him, Romanov and the officer headed for the exit. Wade had turned to follow the cops when Charlotte placed her hand on his arm and stopped him.

"While you're tracking Brett Gamble, if you learn anything about Dinah that I should know, will you tell me?" she asked quietly.

"What do you suspect?"

"I don't know." She smiled sadly. "I'm just wondering what might be going on that I'm unaware of." Her eyes, already red from exhaustion, became shiny with unshed tears. "Dinah and I were so close when we were little, but over the years—the last four or five, especially— we grew apart. It took what happened tonight for me to realize I hardly know her."

Wade wanted to help her, but the request made him uneasy. "I'm a bounty hunter. I look at the details of a case only to the extent that it helps me do my job so I can recover a fugitive." He shook his head. "I won't spy on your sister. You need to hire a private investigator for that."

She kept her hand on his arm. "Do you have any brothers or sisters?"

Wade thought of the Ryan clan: Connor, Danny and Hayley. He and the two younger Ryans—Danny and Hayley—had gone to school together. They'd helped each other through tough times and now they worked together at Range River Bail Bonds. Technically, Wade did not have any siblings. Not related by blood. But the Ryans truly were his family. "Yes," he answered. "I have two brothers and a sister."

"If one of them were in trouble, involved in something bad, wouldn't you want to know so you could help them? I don't mean help them escape the law. I mean help them to be safe, to get their life back together, to hang on to some bit of dignity."

Yes. If any of the Ryans was in trouble, he would want someone to tell him.

Wade drew in a breath and blew it out. "If I learn anything about Dinah that you should know, I'll tell you about it. But only on the condition that you promise to stay vigilant until the criminals we're looking for are caught. And you need to make sure your sister is careful, too."

"Agreed." Charlotte offered him a tired but grateful smile.

Wade found himself drawn into that smile and it was a challenge to look away.

"Come on—let's go," Dinah called out to Charlotte.

Ethan was no longer by Dinah's side. Presumably, he'd gone home for the night. But the security manager was there to provide the sisters an escort.

"Thank you," Charlotte said softly to Wade, before turning and walking toward Dinah.

The bounty hunter let his gaze linger on her for a moment. Even with the resort security team keeping an eye on her, he couldn't help feeling she wasn't completely safe. There were always moments when a person was vulnerable.

He headed for his truck, determined to do everything he could to find the kidnappers and get them off the streets. Only then would he be convinced that Charlotte was truly safe.

THREE

"That's him." Wade pointed at the image on Romanov's electronic tablet. "That's Brett Gamble's accomplice."

It was early in the morning the day after the attack. Shortly after awakening, Wade had received a text from the detective asking him to come to the police station to look at mug shots. He'd grabbed a couple of coffee drinks and huckleberry muffins on his way to the meeting.

Upon receipt of her gifted coffee and muffin, the detective had given him a suspicious frown.

"Not trying to butter you up," he'd said while taking a chair across from her desk. "I needed some breakfast and my mom didn't raise me to be rude."

That actually got him a slight chuckle in response, something he'd never seen the serious-minded detective do before. She'd taken a sip of her brew. "Mocha. Good call. Thanks."

She was sipping her coffee again as she looked at the mug shot that Wade had indicated. "Trey Murphy. Out on parole for armed robbery after serving six years in prison. Looks like he'll be going right back in." She picked up a desk phone, punched in some numbers and then requested officers to go to Murphy's last known address and arrest him.

"Do you really think he'll be there?" Wade asked between sips of coffee.

She shrugged. "A bold criminal is not necessarily a smart one."

A police scanner was audible in her office at low volume. Wade heard a couple of transmissions, one of an officer making a traffic stop and another of an officer reporting that she was back in service after a meal break. He knew that he likely wouldn't hear the dispatch of officers to check on Murphy. A call like that would go out via cell phone messaging on the patrol car's computer so eavesdroppers couldn't hear.

"I went by Gamble's house after I left our meeting at the resort last night," Wade said after taking a bite of his muffin. "A couple of your officers were there, watching the place, but they wouldn't let me in."

Romanov nodded. "Good. I'm glad to hear it."

The detective and her husband had moved to Range River from California a little over a year ago. The first attempts by the bounty hunters from Wade's office to work with her had not gone well. She'd been wary that they would disrupt her investigations and she had at first refused to assist them when they worked pursuits that intersected with her cases. Slowly, over the last few months, the bounty hunters had proved their professionalism and she'd warmed up to them. Somewhat.

"I know you won't tell me what your officers found inside Gamble's home." Wade tapped the lid on his paper coffee cup. "But would you at least let me know if it looks like he cleared the place out? I need to know if he planned ahead and could be anywhere, or if he's in the middle of a panic run and likely has to stay nearby because he's low on resources."

. The detective leaned back in her chair. "Before I answer that, let me remind you that your job is to capture bail jumpers, not to run your own police investigation."

"Yes, ma'am." His job was simply to capture fugitives. But sometimes in the course of doing that job, he got caught up in broader criminal situations.

"If I find out that you intentionally withheld information from this police department and delayed the capture of Brett Gamble—or Trey Murphy—so that you could be the one to make the arrest and earn your bounty hunting fee, you and I are going to have a serious problem."

Wade had heard various versions of this speech from her before. But this time she sounded a little less concerned about that happening.

"Understood," he said. If the police captured a bail jumper, the bounty hunter didn't earn any money. Which meant bounty hunters could be motivated to put their own financial gain ahead of public safety. Range River bounty hunters didn't do that. But other bounty hunters sometimes did.

"I really want Gamble locked up before he can endanger anyone else," Wade said. Collecting the recovery fee would be a second-level priority. Whether he was the one to put cuffs on the guy, or the police were the ones to do it, didn't really matter. Not in this case.

"All right, I'll tell you what we found." Romanov tossed her empty coffee cup into the trash can beside her desk. "The front door at Gamble's house was unlocked when officers got there. They observed muddy footprints leading from the entrance to the master bedroom, where the closet door was left open and a safe was also left open. It was empty, of course."

"So he likely grabbed whatever valuables he had—probably cash and guns—from the safe and got out of there in a hurry," Wade said, thinking out loud. "His plans for whatever he meant to do to Charlotte, under the mistaken impression that she was Dinah, went sideways and now he's in a panic. That might make him a little easier to find."

"Let's hope that's true."

"Now that we've got Trey Murphy identified as the accomplice, will you show his mug shot to Dinah to see if she recognizes him?" Wade asked. "And then will you tell me what she said?"

Romanov arched an auburn eyebrow. "Are you starting to think I work for you?"

"No, ma'am."

Wade got to his feet, ready to take his leave, when an officer stepped into Romanov's office. "Detective, a call just came into the 9-1-1 center from Charlotte Halstead. She says her sister, Dinah, is missing."

Wade's heart clenched.

Romanov was on her feet in an instant. "Let's go!" she called out to the squad room as she headed for the door.

Wade grabbed his phone and tapped the screen. Charlotte had given him her number last night.

She picked up immediately. "Wade! Dinah is gone. Something has happened to her." Her words were oddly spaced, as if she were gasping for air.

"Take a breath," he said, managing to sound calmer than he felt. "Did someone break into your condo?" He imagined the two assailants from last night's attack reappearing in her life and terrifying her again. "Did they hurt you? Are you okay?"

"I'm all right." She started crying and Wade gripped his phone tighter.

"Can you come over here?" she asked after getting hold of her emotions enough to speak clearly. *"Please?"*

He was already out the door and striding toward his truck. "On my way."

Even without the details, Wade knew Charlotte was much too close to danger. He would do whatever he had to, to make certain she wasn't caught up in violence again.

The resort condos were built in Craftsman style and positioned to have dramatic views of Wolf Lake. Wade easily picked out Charlotte's residence. There were cops in front of it and a police forensic team just now walking inside. Romanov had arrived ahead of Wade, and he assumed she was inside with the Halstead family.

Torn between the desire to barge in and see for himself that Charlotte was okay, and the awareness that Romanov might ice him out of her investigation completely if he actually did that, Wade finally sent Charlotte a text letting her know that he was waiting outside.

She immediately replied, telling him to come in. Permission enough. Wade would show the text to the detective if she got mad at him for entering her crime scene.

As expected, the officer on the front step stopped him. But Charlotte, her eyes swollen and red, saw Wade through the open door and waved him in.

Romanov was in the midst of interviewing the Halstead parents and Ethan as they all stood in the living room. The detective shot the bounty hunter a disapproving look, but otherwise continued her questioning without missing a beat.

Kandace Halstead, however, was distracted by Wade's arrival. "What is the bounty hunter doing here?" she asked weakly. Her features were slack and Wade noted the stunned and confused expression in her eyes.

"He can help, Mom," Charlotte said. "He has connections in the criminal world."

When she put it that way, Wade couldn't blame Mrs. Halstead for being wary of him.

"It will speed things up to have the police *and* a bounty hunter searching for Dinah," Charlotte continued. "Having his help could get Dinah home faster."

Mrs. Halstead gave her daughter a curt nod of agreement. Beside her, Mr. Halstead rubbed at his eyes with a handkerchief and then blew his nose. Ethan, red-faced and shiny-eyed, had his arms wrapped tightly across his chest as if trying to hold himself together.

"When and how did you discover that your sister was missing?" Romanov asked Charlotte, refusing to have her interview derailed.

"After I woke up and went downstairs to start a pot of coffee, I knocked on the door of the ground-floor bedroom to see if Dinah wanted some, and she wasn't there." The last few words came out breathy, with Charlotte struggling to speak. She took a moment to compose herself and continued. "Her purse was on the nightstand. And her phone." Charlotte's voice cracked and she cleared her throat.

"At that moment I *knew* something was wrong. Even if she'd left to get some breakfast in one of the resort dining facilities or gone back to her apartment, she wouldn't have left her phone behind." Charlotte took a deep breath. "I looked around on the property for her, hoping that I was overreacting and she was somewhere on the grounds. But I couldn't find her anywhere." Tears began to roll down her cheeks.

The sight triggered a twisting sensation in Wade's gut, strengthening his determination to find Gamble. Someone must have broken into Charlotte's home at some point while she was asleep and vulnerable. The thought of that was beyond unacceptable.

"Did you hear anything last night?" Romanov asked.

Charlotte shook her head. "I was so upset about being kidnapped and chased that I was afraid I wouldn't be able to fall asleep. But I did. Quickly. I slept straight through until this morning."

"We went through all the video security feeds for the property and couldn't see her anywhere," Ethan added, his voice sounding tight.

"You live on the resort property, as well?" Romanov asked him.

Ethan shook his head. "No. I live a few blocks away. I came here as soon as I learned Dinah was missing."

A crime scene tech stepped into the living room from the bedroom where Dinah had been staying. "No sign of forced entry," he said to Romanov. "There's a slider door that opens to a patio. We found it unlocked and closed, but the screen door had been left pushed open. We're lifting prints right now. Also, a small table on the patio was knocked over. Looks like there was a potted plant on it that's lying beside it now, broken."

"The door could have been inadvertently left unlocked," Romanov mused. "Or someone could have had a key."

"What happened to the security employee who was supposed to be watching this place?" Wade meant to ask Charlotte the question quietly, but apparently Romanov overheard.

"Yes, wasn't someone from the security team supposed to keep an eye on you and your sister last night?" she asked Charlotte.

"I already talked to the guy," Ethan interjected. "He admitted that he pulled up a chair and sat out front, looking toward the lake. He claims he got up and walked around the building every hour, but I'm not sure I believe him."

"How is it that there would be no security video of the rear exterior of this building?" Romanov pressed.

"We've got cameras scattered across the property, but there are blind spots, nevertheless," Arthur Halstead answered. "I now know that the backside of this condo is not visible to the cameras. I didn't realize that before." He wiped his eyes with the handkerchief again and cleared his throat before saying, "You are welcome to view as much security video as you want. Beyond that, I'll give you access to every inch of the resort buildings and the grounds. I'll arrange for you to interview my employees. Anything you need, just tell me."

Romanov nodded. "I'll start with having a couple of officers talk to your security employees and we'll go from there."

The detective left and Wade walked out behind her, figuring Charlotte and her family would want their privacy. He considered how to best start searching for Gamble and hopefully find Dinah. Or, alternately, he could set his sights on finding Dinah and hope that also led him to Gamble. Same goal, but the methods would be a little different.

"I need to speak with you." Charlotte caught up with Wade, stopping him on the footpath in front of her home.

Arthur and Kandace passed by on their way to the main building, both of them talking on their phones. Ethan stopped long enough to give Charlotte a side-hug before continuing on to the main building, as well.

"Let me work with you," Charlotte said to Wade when everyone else was out of earshot.

The bounty hunter stared at her and grasped for a polite way to tell her, *No. Absolutely not.* She was frantic and scared and had no idea what she was asking him.

"I already know the police won't let me work with them," Charlotte added, correctly reading his hesitation. "And the resort security team is here to keep guests safe. They aren't going to go searching for my sister."

Wade thought of a few choice things he had to say about the resort's security team, but decided to keep them to himself.

"Charlotte, *you* could be a target. An intentional one, this time." Wade was determined not to get pulled in by the pleading expression in her eyes. "Between what happened last night and now your sister going missing, nobody knows what's going on or what the motivations are behind it. The best thing would be for you to stay with your parents until Dinah is back home."

The expression in Charlotte's eyes shifted from pleading into something stronger. "You told me that you work differently from the police. And that your success at least in part comes from gathering information from people who won't talk to the cops."

Wade nodded. "That's true."

"Well, it's not just criminals who don't want to talk to cops. I know plenty of people in this town who care more about maintaining their reputations than helping anyone else. They'd give minimum information to the police, if they'd talk to them at all. They normally wouldn't even consider talking to a bounty hunter. But, because they know me or my family, they might give you the time of day if I were with you."

Her argument made sense. Wade found that alarming. He couldn't take Charlotte Halstead with him while he was working a case, could he?

"You'll get faster results with me along." Charlotte apparently sensed that her argument had found a foothold. "I can give you ideas on where Dinah spends her time and who her friends are. Together, we can find my sister. And your fugitive," she added.

Wade gazed down into her stubborn blue eyes and decided it wouldn't be an easy thing to talk her out of this idea, or anything else she set her mind to.

"I can't let you do it," he said. "It's not safe."

"It's not like I'm going to try to act like a bounty hunter or do anything dangerous or foolish. I just want to help you talk to people so that you can find my sister and the criminals who kidnapped me."

She might search for information about Dinah whether she was working alongside him or not. Wade would definitely rather keep an eye on her than have her out looking for Dinah alone and making herself an easy target.

He could only hope that after a few hours of bounty hunter–style grunt work—involving people with hostile attitudes, time wasted pursuing dead-end leads and having to untangle the flat-out lies they would be told—she'd get tired of it and want to go home.

"All right," he finally said, not feeling entirely comfortable with his decision. "Let's get started."

"It's only 10:00 a.m. I'm not sure we can get a whole lot accomplished this early in the day. Most of my informants are still asleep," Wade said.

Charlotte watched him complete and send a text before setting his phone on his truck's center console. They were parked in the resort garage, making plans to start searching for Dinah. Charlotte fought to ignore the coffee headache tightening the nerves at the base of her skull. Once she'd realized her sister was missing, she'd forgotten all about getting her morning caffeine. But her head was reminding her about it right now.

"I managed to get hold of a few contacts last night to ask if any of them knew Brett Gamble," he continued. "None of them did, but they said they'd ask around. It might take a little while to hear back from them, but at least that ball is already rolling."

"These informants are mostly criminals, I suppose," Charlotte asked.

Wade nodded. "In this case, all of them."

"I assume they help you for the money. How do you know they aren't lying to you? Feeding you false information so they'll get paid?"

Wade shrugged. "It happens sometimes. But over time those people are easy to weed out. Now, what kind of leads can *you* give me to help us find your sister?"

Charlotte opened her mouth, but before she could speak he held up a hand to stop her. "I should tell you that the cops will go through the phone company to try and get a look at your sister's contact list and recent activity. We don't want to waste time duplicating their efforts. I'm not interested in the names of her friends that everyone knows about. I'm looking for something different."

"Like what?"

"I don't know yet. You tell me. Has she made any new friends recently? Maybe a man she hasn't told her boyfriend about?"

"No." Charlotte shook her head. And then found herself adding, "At least, not that I know of." Given the circumstances, the reminder that she and her twin weren't close carried an especially sharp sting. She shook her head, angry with herself. When they went their separate ways after high school, they'd let go of each other. Why had she let that happen?

"I couldn't miss hearing about Dinah's problems with drugs and alcohol in college. What can you tell me about that?"

"Nothing. I only learned about it when you did."

He didn't believe her. She could tell by his lifted brows and the slight tilt of his head. She could hardly blame him. What kind of parents would keep a secret like that from the rest of their family? From their other child? She knew the answer almost immediately. Parents whose foremost concern was their reputation and public persona. No wonder Dinah had turned out to be so much that way. Overly concerned about what everyone thought of her. Compelled to always look perfect. To be perfect.

Charlotte could only wonder what other secrets her family was keeping from her.

"Dinah said she quit college because she was bored, and I believed her."

As a tremor of worry and fear passed through her, Charlotte turned to gaze out of her side window, taking the opportunity to wipe away the tears forming in her eyes. She'd convinced Wade that she would be of help to him if he let her tag along as he searched for Dinah and Gamble. She refused to spend her time with him crying.

She shifted her thoughts toward her sister's recent activities. At least, the ones she knew about. She dug through her purse for her phone and tapped open a social media app. "Dinah likes to post pictures of herself all over town, not just at the resort," Charlotte told Wade. "Here she is at Club Sapphire over on Indigo Street. She's spent a lot of time there lately."

Wade glanced at the photo, a selfie of Dinah with a wall of deep blue glass behind her. "Okay, good. Let's head over there." He slid on a pair of dark sunglasses and started the engine.

"It'll be closed right now," Charlotte said.

"Somebody will be there getting things ready to open up tonight. Your sister's a local celebrity. I'm sure at least some of the employees have paid attention when she's been in there. Maybe somebody noticed something helpful."

He pulled out of the parking garage and drove northward, toward the river that gave the town its name, and the historic street that ran alongside the north bank and was home to handcraft shops, trendy clothing stores, nightclubs and restaurants.

As Wade drove, Charlotte scrolled through a couple of different social media accounts, searching for Dinah's posts.

"While you're looking at those, pay attention to the people around her," Wade said with a glance in Charlotte's direction. "So if we run across any of them later, you'll recognize them."

Charlotte studied the photos, doing her best to commit what she saw to memory.

They arrived at Indigo Street a short time later. The old cobblestone road was now a pedestrian-only thoroughfare, so they parked in a municipal lot at the end of the street and headed toward the main hub of activities.

As expected, Club Sapphire was closed. Wade led the way around the nightclub to the delivery entrance in the back.

He rang the bell and added a couple of loud knocks on the door. A few moments later, a man in jeans and a T-shirt and wearing a heavy cleaning apron threw open the door. "Can I help you?" His gaze strayed to Charlotte and stayed there. He squinted slightly, looking confused.

Uncertain how to respond, she nervously reached up to smooth her hair.

"We'd like to talk to you about a missing woman," Wade said. "Her name is Dinah Halstead. Do you know her?"

The man broke his gaze away from Charlotte and

then laughed self-consciously. "Of course." He smiled at Charlotte. "I heard Dinah had an identical twin sister and that would obviously be you. Kind of threw me off at first."

Charlotte had experienced similar reactions before. Especially when they were younger, people regularly mistook one Halstead sister for the other. And thanks to her family's ownership of the Wolf Lake Resort, she was used to complete strangers knowing who she was. "I'm Charlotte," she said, figuring this was her opportunity to step up and show Wade that she could get someone to talk to them. "This is Wade Fast Horse. And we could really use your help."

The man opened the door a little wider and ushered them inside. "Stuart Dees. Officially, I'm the night manager. In reality, I'm the guy who does a little bit of everything." He gestured toward his apron. "The day manager called in sick this morning, so I was asked to come help out and make sure things were under control. Normally, I'd be home sleeping right now."

The main expanse of the club was in shadows. Stuart led the way to a section of the bar where circles of light shone down from low-hanging fixtures. Through an open door behind the bar, Charlotte saw into a kitchen where three or four people were bustling around cleaning and doing food prep work.

"So, you said Dinah's missing?" Stuart pulled out a couple of barstools for them to sit down on while he walked around to stand behind the bar. He picked up a mug and took a couple of sips from it. "I'm sorry to hear that. She's a nice lady. What happened?"

Charlotte started to speak, but was surprised to find

herself getting choked up. Her emotions were still close to the surface and she quickly realized she wouldn't be able to describe finding her sister missing without starting to cry again. Her feelings of fear and sorrow were made even stronger in this place where her sister had been enjoying herself only a couple of nights ago.

Wade stepped in and gave a brief summary of the morning's events, leaving out the attack on Charlotte last night.

Stuart shook his head. "That's horrible. How can I help you?"

"Tell us who she hangs out with when she's in here," Wade said.

Stuart's expression shifted subtly and he chewed his lower lip for a moment. "Sorry, but I can't say that I've paid attention to that. When I'm here, I'm busy working. Know what I mean?"

Charlotte knew what he meant. But she didn't believe him. She figured he observed a lot more than he was admitting to.

"We have good reason to believe Dinah's in grave danger," she said. "Maybe you could just give us a single name that would send us in the right direction."

He shrugged. "Sorry, can't help you."

The surge of frustration Charlotte felt was maddening. She wanted to reach out and shake some sense into the guy, but realized that probably wasn't a good idea.

Wade calmly got to his feet. Charlotte did, too. And then Wade handed over his business card.

"'Bounty hunter'?" Stuart read off the card, looking up with a surprised expression.

Wade nodded. "And like Charlotte said, we believe her sister is in serious danger."

Stuart pursed his lips together as if considering something, and for a moment it looked like he might help them. But then his expression shuttered again. He came around from behind the bar and walked them back to the delivery door. "I hope you find her."

"He's noticed who she hangs out with when she's here. He just won't tell us," Charlotte fumed as they stepped outside and the door closed behind them.

Wade nodded at her and then reached for his phone. "Happens all the time."

"Doesn't it bother you?" Her head was starting to throb again.

"It doesn't help for me to get upset," Wade said while looking down at his phone's screen. "He might think it over and decide to call me later. That sometimes happens. Don't get discouraged. We're just getting started." He glanced up at her. "Looks like I've got an informant checking in. Let's see what he's got to say."

While he took the call, Charlotte walked around aimlessly behind the nightclub, hoping to burn off some of her aggravation and impatiently waiting for him to end the call and tell her what he'd learned.

She walked one direction and then the other, before noticing the back of a diner with the words *fresh hot coffee served all day* painted across the brick wall. She hadn't gotten any coffee this morning, and while it seemed like a petty concern in the light of things, she nevertheless thought caffeine might help her headache and ease her aggravation.

Wade was still engaged in his call. Rather than interrupt him and ask what he wanted to drink, she decided to bring him back a standard coffee with sugar and cream and hope he liked it. Figuring she should send him a text so he'd know where she'd gone, she reached into her purse for her phone. As she rounded the corner of the building where the coffee shop was located, she heard a noise behind her. Assuming it was Wade catching up with her, she started to turn. She felt a sudden, sharp pain on the back of her head, and then, darkness.

FOUR

Where is she going?

Wade kept his gaze fixed on the corner of the building where he'd seen Charlotte disappear just a moment ago. He was still on the phone call with his informant, who had so far only offered general information about Brett Gamble, none of which was news to Wade.

While staying on the call, the bounty hunter began to follow his temporary working partner.

As soon as he spotted the word *coffee* painted on the bricks above an image of a steaming cup on the backside of the building in front of him, he knew exactly where Charlotte was going and why. He breathed in the rich aroma as he moved closer, figuring he could do with a caffeine reload, as well.

The sound of scuffling footsteps beside the building, just ahead of him and out of sight, caught his attention. A heavy feeling of unease quickly dropped over him.

"I'll call you back," he said into the phone, cutting off his informant midsentence. He shoved the device into the holder on his belt, just as he heard the soft echo of a sound that sounded like a woman's gasp.

He hoped he was mistaken. It could be some ordinary sound from the next street over carrying down the passageway and into the alley. But Wade had learned a long time ago to anticipate the worst and save hoping for the best for some other time. When exactly that time would come, he had no idea. Wade didn't think of himself as a pessimist. He was a realist.

The thought of Charlotte in danger already had his heart pumping and his legs moving faster.

His main worry for her had been that she might be caught in the cross fire when the bad guys came after Dinah again. Maybe he was wrong. Maybe this time they'd intentionally come after *her*.

"Charlotte!" He shouted her name as he cleared the corner of the building and his heart fell at the sight in front of him. At the far end of the narrow drive, where it met the intersecting street, last night's attackers, bail jumper Brett Gamble and the accomplice now identified as Trey Murphy, had Charlotte. Even more alarming, it looked as if Charlotte was unconscious.

Gamble held her by the arms, Murphy had her legs, and they were about to swing her into the back seat of an idling sedan.

"Stop!" Wade yelled, summoning every bit of strength he had to race toward them.

The kidnappers moved faster, with Gamble shoving the upper half of Charlotte's body inside the vehicle and then letting go to race around the back of the car and head for the driver's seat.

Wade's blood ran cold. They were going to get away. With Charlotte!

But then her body twisted, as though she'd been startled awake. She twisted again, harder, deliberately, aiming kicks at Murphy's head as he kept his grip on her legs and tried to force the lower half of her body into the back seat of the vehicle.

Good job, Charlotte! Wade thought, proud of her for putting up such a strong fight. *Hold on!* He was almost to her.

Murphy let go and stopped trying to manhandle her the rest of the way into the car. Instead, he turned his body so that he was facing Wade. Using the weight of his own body, the thug backed into Charlotte, sitting on her to hold her in place. Then he reached for a gun and fired at Wade.

The bounty hunter had just reached the front of the diner and he dived behind a waist-high hedge in front of a plate-glass window. Bullets flew around him, chipping the brick building, punching holes in the steel rain gutters, and finally striking the large window and sending down a rainfall of shattered glass.

Wade was vaguely aware of the small shards scraping and scratching the back of his neck as he crouched behind the hedge, but he kept his attention focused on Charlotte and the assailants.

Behind him, from inside the diner, he heard screams and shouts and the scraping sounds of hastily moved chairs and heavy thud of tables tipping over. The patrons and employees were likely trying to get away from the window or take cover. Good. He figured at least one of them was already calling 9-1-1.

But he couldn't wait for the police. Any second now, Murphy would turn his attention from Wade back to Charlotte. With his gun pointed at her, she'd have no choice but to comply and pull her legs into the car so they could make their getaway.

The criminals had likely hoped to grab her in as low-key a manner as possible—at least, as low-key as it was possible to carry out something like that in broad daylight. Knock her unconscious in an alleyway, hustle her to a waiting vehicle, and figure that anyone casually glancing in their direction might not recognize that they were witnessing an abduction.

But now there was no longer any reason for the kidnappers to be cautious.

And for all Wade knew, they had no particular reason to keep Charlotte alive for very long. Maybe she was just a pawn in some kind of attempt to get money owed them by Dinah. Maybe Charlotte was valuable to them alive for only a short time. And after a short time, they'd do whatever they had to so they could get rid of her quickly.

He didn't dare shoot back at Murphy. The creep was still so close to Charlotte that he was leaning back onto her. A bullet sent in that direction could get her killed. But maybe Wade could take out the tires. At least one of them. Something that would slow them down, make them realize that they couldn't flee fast enough to escape law enforcement if they kept fighting to kidnap Charlotte. Just like Wade, they must be anticipating the cops' arrival at any moment now.

Wade scanned the area, hoping for a clear shot with no innocents in the way. It looked good. He aimed for the front passenger side tire, flicked off the safety, was just about to pull the trigger when he heard an approaching engine and a car drove past.

Wade held his fire, and to his horror, Murphy turned to Charlotte and started lifting his gun to point it at her. But before the perp could take aim, she landed a kick in the center of his gut. Clearly caught off guard, the kidnapper crumpled in pain. Charlotte grabbed her chance, shoved him aside as he was doubled over and pressed past him as she climbed out of the car and sprinted for cover.

Wade sprang to his feet and shoved through the hedge, angling toward Charlotte, who was looking around frantically as if uncertain which way to go.

Bracing himself for a shot that could come from the criminals at any moment, the bounty hunter cleared the expanse between himself and Charlotte and then leaped at her while twisting his body so that when they landed he would take the brunt of the impact. Holding her tightly, he continued the roll until they were behind a cement planter surrounding a tree in front of the dry cleaner next to the diner.

Bang! Bang!

Bullets struck the edge of the planter, sending chunks and smaller fragments of cement flying.

Wade got to his hands and knees, shielding Charlotte's body with his own as he inched forward to take a look. He assumed it was Murphy shooting at them, and if the kidnapper was advancing on them, Wade had to do something to get Charlotte to safety. "Get ready to run back toward the alley," he said without turning to look at her. "Head for my truck as fast as you can." He reached into his pocket for his key fob. Keeping his gaze focused toward the danger, he tossed it back in her direction.

"What about you?" she asked in a shaky voice.

"Don't worry about me." Wade could look after himself. It was a skill he'd picked up at an early age. After his dad vanished and his mom worked all hours of the day.

Still crouched, he pushed himself up onto his toes, readying to spring forward toward the shooter, figuring this was a case where the best defense was an offensive move and hoping to gain the upper hand by surprising Murphy.

Bang! Bang!

One more quick look around the planter before he made his move had gotten two more gunshots fired in his direction. But in that instant, he'd also been able to see that the kidnapper had shut the rear passenger door and moved toward the front of the car. A small ember of hope flared to life within him. *They're giving up!* It looked like they weren't going to keep trying to take Charlotte. At least, not right now.

Murphy yelled something. Wade couldn't make out the words over the rumble of the car's engine and he didn't much care what the jerk had to say anyway. The kidnapper's shouting was followed by the slamming of a car door and the growl of an engine after its accelerator had been punched. Tires squealed. Wade raised his head to get a clearer view.

The assailant's car was speeding away. "They're going," Wade said, watching the car for as long as possible while reaching for his phone to call Detective Romanov directly. But before he could tap the screen to make the connection, he heard a sound behind him that caught his attention.

He turned as Charlotte, who'd held herself together despite her obvious terror, began working her throat as she fought to hold back sobs. Finally, she burst into tears.

Wade was only too familiar with the feeling the moment after a terrifying ordeal when you realized you were safe and all the emotions you'd choked down while you fought to survive clawed their way to the surface. Thugs like Murphy and Gamble didn't just commit physical crimes. They did things that left behind emotional scars, some that lasted a lifetime. Knowing people like them existed was the motivation behind Wade doing what he did for a living. Taking criminals off the streets. Protecting innocent people who simply wanted to go about their daily lives.

"Everything's okay." Wade worked to settle his own intense emotions so that his voice would be calm and steady. "They're gone and you're all right."

She fought her way through a couple of ragged breaths, staring down at the ground where they were both still sitting. "They called me by name." Her words sounded scratchy and squeezed by emotion. "This time they knew it was me and not Dinah."

Her words confirmed his new fear. Now the kidnappers were after Charlotte, specifically. Wade had heard the threat Gamble directed to Dinah when he and Charlotte were hiding on the loading dock. Clearly, Gamble had mistaken Charlotte for her identical twin. But now things had changed and he and his partner had targeted Charlotte. Why? What had changed? And what was the bigger story here?

"I don't understand any of this." Charlotte shook her head and then lifted her face, settling a searching gaze on Wade. Tear tracks marked the sides of her cheeks. Her shoulder-length blond hair, normally neatly parted on the side and tucked behind her ears, now fell across her face in twists and tangles. Before he knew what he was doing, Wade reached out to brush some of the errant strands aside.

His fingertips brushed the soft skin of her forehead and temples and he told himself he was just trying to make it easier for her to see, even as he felt the unexpected catch in his breath at the flush in her cheeks.

Awareness of what was going on hit him like a snap and he drew back his hand. This was not happening. He wouldn't let it. They were temporary working partners. She was a woman who needed the help and protection he could offer. That was all.

Although, she'd just now done a pretty magnificent job of protecting herself.

The thought brought a return of that catch in his breath.

Determined to get his thoughts—and the accompanying feelings—under control, Wade leaned back and got to his feet, all the while schooling the expression on his face to something appropriately serious. He didn't want to think about what might have been written plainly on his face moments ago. Something ridiculous, no doubt.

"Let me help you up." He extended his hand. When Charlotte grasped it, when she touched him, that feeling was there again. A gentle warmth that was something beyond simply the temperature of her skin. But this time Wade was ready for it and he immediately cut off the unwelcome feeling of connection, turning his attention from Charlotte to their surroundings.

Unfortunately, it took another few moments for him to realize he still needed to let go of her hand.

Sirens wailed at the end of the street, accompanied by the flashing red and blue lights of police cars speeding in their direction. People slowly emerged from the diner and the dry cleaner and several other businesses on the street after apparently taking cover inside.

"We need to have a paramedic check you over as soon as an ambulance gets here."

Charlotte blew out a deep breath. "I'm fine. I have

a headache, but I had a headache before they hit me on the back of the head. And I never got my coffee."

Wade gritted his teeth. The thought of someone striking her like that soured his stomach. And it sharpened his determination to get the kidnappers off the streets. "Well, you still need to get checked out. Maybe go to the hospital for X-rays."

"I will if that seems necessary. Otherwise, I don't want to waste time on it." She crossed her arms over her chest and gave him a steadfast look that took him by surprise as the cop cars rolled up to them. "We need to keep looking for my sister."

Despite his best intentions to keep his emotions in check, Wade still felt the flutter of something warm and not altogether unpleasant in the center of his chest. Maybe Charlotte Halstead wasn't the soft, spoiled daughter of wealth that he'd thought she was. There was no denying that the woman had backbone. Hopefully, it would continue to help keep her alive.

"We were able to get the plate numbers off the perps' car thanks to a couple nearby security cameras," Detective Romanov said. "It was stolen, of course, but patrol will be on the lookout for it. And I've got a unit canvassing the neighborhood where it was stolen searching for potential witnesses and seeing if anybody there has outdoor security video."

Charlotte nodded her understanding. Other than that, she had no idea what to say. Tracking criminals was not a normal part of her life.

She and Wade were in the detective's office a couple of hours after the attack outside the coffee shop. The detective had arrived on the scene shortly after the initial responding officers, where she'd conducted quick interviews with Charlotte and Wade.

Now, while two other police detectives along with patrol officers interviewed diner patrons and followed up on related leads, Romanov was ready to talk to Charlotte and Wade again.

"What exactly did Gamble and Murphy say to you?" Romanov asked.

It took Charlotte a moment to rouse herself to answer. Despite Wade getting her a very large and very strong espresso drink with lots of chocolate in it, she was exhausted and her mind was unfocused. It had to be the surge of adrenaline and subsequent drop that had her feeling an edgy combination of sleepy and jittery. But at least she had no symptoms of concussion and her headache had finally gone away. The coffee drink and a couple of ibuprofen had eased the throbbing pain. At the moment, she just had to make sure she didn't lean the tender knot on the back of her head against the chair or she'd quickly be reminded that not too long ago she'd been hit hard enough to lose consciousness.

That was a creepy thing to think about and she didn't want to dwell on it.

"As I've mentioned before, one minute I was walking to the diner and turning around because I thought I heard Wade walking up behind me, and the next thing I knew, I was being carried by my hands and feet. I recognized Gamble first because he was closest to my face." Charlotte stopped for a moment, as the stark terror she'd felt in that instant became immediate and real to her even though she was safe inside the police department. For a few seconds, she couldn't breathe.

"Take your time," Wade said gently.

She glanced at him, taking comfort in the determined yet compassionate expression on his face.

"Breathe," he added.

Filling her lungs and blowing out the air a couple of times did seem to help.

"When I recognized Gamble, I tried to break free of his grip and I shouted, 'I'm not Dinah!'" Charlotte resumed. "He said, 'I know, Charlotte. This time it's *you* we want.'"

Romanov leaned forward, resting her elbows on her desk. "What else did he say? Or the other one, Murphy, did he say anything?"

Charlotte shook her head, carefully, just to make sure it didn't start hurting again. "Everything else was just them threatening to kill me if I didn't cooperate with them and them ordering me to get into the car." She swallowed thickly. "I was pretty sure they planned to kill me eventually anyway, so I fought back. I escaped. Murphy yelled something before they drove away, but I couldn't hear clearly enough to understand it."

The detective turned to Wade.

"Same," he said. "I could tell the guy was yelling, but that old car had a bad muffler. It drowned out his words."

"Why do you think they didn't just shoot you in the passage beside the coffee shop and be done with it?" Romanov asked.

It was a harsh question. But not one Charlotte hadn't already asked herself. "Murphy could have killed me when he snuck into my SUV thinking I was Dinah. He didn't. But at the same time, both men seemed willing to use lethal force to make sure I didn't get away." She sighed. "Gamble said Dinah owed him. He had to mean she owed him money as opposed to, say, owing him a favor. Maybe he meant to grab me to get money, too."

"You mean he wants to hold one or both of you for ransom?" Wade asked.

"I don't know what I mean. I'm confused and I'm just doing my best to think of things that could help us figure this out."

"Do you think the Invaders could have a part in this?" Wade asked the detective. "Attempts at making quick money and use of violence are right up their alley."

"Invaders?" Charlotte asked, thinking maybe she'd misheard him. "What does that mean?"

"They're a criminal motorcycle gang that operates in and around Range River. They're involved in everything from illicit drug sales to auto theft to strong-arm robbery and crimes beyond that. More than one member has faced murder charges."

A sound that was a combination of a cough and a laugh came out of Charlotte's mouth. Because she could hardly believe what he was saying. "You're telling me that Range River has an outlaw biker gang running around?" She shook her head. "I've never heard anything about it."

"How closely do you follow crime?" Wade asked.

It was a fair question. "Until now, not too closely. I'd catch news headlines, but that's about it."

"They're not above kidnapping for ransom, extortion, blackmail. Whatever could be the motivation for these attacks, I could see them being involved in it." He turned to the detective. "Maybe we should take a look in that direction. See if Dinah's being held at the gang house out on Tributary Road."

"The police will deal with the Invaders. Not you."

Romanov focused a hard stare toward Wade. "Don't try to talk to any of the gang members. I am explicitly telling you to stay away from them."

"You've got an ongoing investigation into them, don't you?" Wade said.

The detective didn't respond.

"Okay." Wade nodded. "I understand. If you've got an undercover officer or officers working with them, I don't want to get in the way."

Romanov responded with a sharp nod. "See that you don't."

"Meanwhile, we need to strengthen security for you." Wade shifted his attention to Charlotte.

His gaze, determined and protective, calmed some of the edginess that had her nerves so aggravatingly unbalanced. For a moment she let herself revel in the feeling—the dream, really—of having someone focused on caring for her and looking out for her. Someone she could rely on. Someone who would be there when she needed him to help her feel strong.

But then the moment passed, and she let the dream—because it really was just a dream—go. Charlotte had grown up seeing warm, close families. Some were friends; some were visitors she observed vacationing at the family resort. Their casual connectedness was visible in their body language, in the way they talked to one another, in the inevitable family spats that appeared to be quickly resolved. It was obvious that the various family members really, truly had each other's back.

Charlotte's family was good at keeping up appearances. Over the years there had been countless photos taken of the Halstead family with their blonde twin daughters, everyone looking cozy gathered around fireplaces in the winter or seated on boats on Wolf Lake in the summer. Charlotte would never claim that her parents hadn't taken care of her. They bought everything their daughters could possibly need, and then some. But Arthur and Kandace Halstead were very focused on their resort, on expanding it and increasing bookings not only for individuals but also for large conference events.

That took a lot of energy and a lot of hours in the day, so they needed to be focused and efficient. An extra hug, a few minutes away from the phone or meetings or their laptops to listen to an adolescent girl's worries or fears, was a waste of their precious time.

Charlotte often wondered if the emotional support she'd thought she'd seen in other families was real, or were they faking it, too? She couldn't be sure. But she had discovered a foundation of strength and comfort when she'd come to faith while away at college. And she'd met people through her church and prayer groups who were very supportive.

But even with that experience, she still couldn't bring herself to completely emotionally rely on another person in any situation that truly mattered. Maybe it had always been unreasonable for her to expect anyone else to care about her that much. All she knew was that she'd learned long ago not to get her hopes up. The crash that came when she'd leaned on someone and they'd chosen not to shoulder the burden and instead leave her on her own was just too painful.

She would rely on her faith, and herself, and that was it.

She would rely on the bounty hunter to protect her physically, because he'd proved he could do that. But there was no way she would give in to the pull that tempted her to trust him to be steadfast when she needed someone to lean on.

"We have a security team at the resort who can help keep an eye on me," Charlotte finally said in response to Wade's comment about her needing better protection.

He tilted his head slightly. "They didn't do much for your sister."

"True." What else could she say? At the end of the day, you couldn't pay people to care.

Perhaps the security employee who was supposed to protect the twins had intentionally let Dinah get kidnapped. Maybe he'd been paid off. The thought sent a chill racing across Charlotte's skin and she shivered.

"Until we have a better handle on what's going on, I think you should stay at a secure location." Wade exchanged glances with the detective before turning back to Charlotte. "Connor Ryan, owner of Range River Bail Bonds and my adopted brother, inherited the old Riverside Inn five years ago. The grounds were overgrown and the building dilapidated, but he did some rebuilding and repairs and made it a private residence. He's got state-of-the-art security. We've had people who were in danger stay there before. My mother manages the property, and when necessary, she or Danny or Hayley Ryan move in temporarily to add extra security."

"You're asking me to stay with your brother?"

He offered her the slight boyish smile that completely eased his normally serious expression. It also made Charlotte's stomach do silly little flip-flops for some dumb reason. "I'll be there, too, along with my mom," he said. "It's quite large. Plenty of room. And I hope you like cats and dogs, because Connor's got several of both. He likes to pretend that they aren't actually his, and that some other mysterious person can't resist adopting abandoned animals."

Charlotte knew the building he was talking about. It was a beautiful structure surrounded by tall pines on the southern bank of the Range River. She was vaguely aware that the property had been given a substantial face-lift not too long ago, but she hadn't known the details.

It was a gorgeous location. And after today's attack, Charlotte did feel especially vulnerable. But she'd never laid eyes on Wade Fast Horse until last night, and now he was suggesting she move in with him and a group of strangers? *Bounty hunters*, at that?

"It's not a bad idea," Detective Romanov said. "I've worked with Connor Ryan and his crew for a year now. They're ethical people. I know of at least one woman who, like yourself, was in danger and needed a safe place to stay. She moved to the Riverside Inn until the men who were threatening her life were brought to justice. She told me after the fact that she was very glad she'd made the decision to do that."

Charlotte blew out a sigh. It was time to let go of her hopes that Dinah would be found quickly and things would go back to normal in a day or so. After all that had happened, that didn't seem likely.

Charlotte and Dinah had not been close for a long time. And now that Charlotte knew of her twin's drug and alcohol problems—which had been kept secret, with the possible result of making the situation worse—she was especially frustrated with Dinah and their parents. Why not let a problem like that see the light of day and try to heal it? Was the secretiveness something

Dinah had requested, or was it a case of their parents wanting to put on a good face for the public?

And were these recent terrifying attacks and Dinah's disappearance somehow related to that addiction problem?

In spite of everything, Charlotte loved her sister. Even when she was annoyed by her. She wanted to help Dinah, to rescue her. She wanted to do what she needed to keep herself safe and alive, too. Despite having a paid security team at the resort, it looked like the Range River Bail Bonds crew would be her best choice.

"All right, thank you. I'll stay at the inn," she finally said.

What choice did she have? Her life was in danger, the Wolf Lake Resort was not as secure as she'd thought it was, and she had nowhere else to go.

FIVE

"It looks like a fortress." Charlotte's gaze swept over the stone-and-heavy-timber building in front of her.

"Connor wanted to keep the feel of the original Riverside Inn," Wade responded. "It was designed to withstand harsh weather along with the occasional bandit attack when it was originally built back in the 1880s. The town of Range River afforded the only river crossing for miles around and a lot of tradesmen and merchants with gold or silver on hand stayed at the inn. That made it a tempting target."

Just beyond the building, the Range River flowed by with late-afternoon sunlight glinting on its splashy, riotous surface. Spring had announced its presence with rain and snowmelt resulting from warmer days. The runoff from the surrounding mountains made its way to the river, where it flowed westward toward the Pacific Ocean.

"Well, it's a gorgeous setting."

The resort had a beautiful view of the Wolf Lake and the surrounding mountains, but this particular spot felt cozier and homier to Charlotte. Maybe it was because of the surrounding trees, meandering blackberry vines and the neat redbrick path leading to the oversize front door.

Unlike the lodge, it didn't have an attached parking garage, a large staff and numerous guests wandering around.

In any event, here she was, with a suitcase full of clothes that she'd grabbed on a quick trip to her condo. She'd tried calling her mom and ended up leaving a voice mail with a vague explanation that she didn't feel safe in her condo, so she would be staying with "friends" instead. Any further explanation would have led to her parents questioning her decision. And telling them about the attack would upset them for no reason.

"I messaged my mom, so she's already here and planning to make dinner tonight," Wade said, carrying Charlotte's suitcase as they walked up to the front door.

"She doesn't normally stay here?"

Wade shook his head. "All of us have our own homes. But we've got rooms here for when we need them. Range River Bail Bonds has a storefront office in town—so no bail bond clients ever come out here—but we sometimes meet to discuss strategy here. If we've got an intense case, or a dangerous situation going on, we tend to all move in here and stay until the case or situation is resolved. Connor's generous about letting people visit for a while when they need a safe place to stay. When that happens, some or all of us usually move in to help out."

Wade punched a number into a keypad beside the front door and pushed it open.

They were immediately greeted with the sounds of barking dogs and canine toenails tapping on a wooden floor.

"They don't sound like guard dogs," Charlotte mused.

"Yeah, you'd think a home owned by a bounty hunter would have vicious attack dogs, but no."

The words were barely out of his mouth when they were greeted by several bundles of fur of various colors and sizes. A small white dog with an underbite and hair nearly covering its eyes seemed to be the boldest, and it stepped up to Charlotte, nose quivering, and delightedly sniffed her hand, which Charlotte held out in greeting.

Not wanting the other pups to feel left out, she made certain to hold her hand out to each of them, too, as she brushed by them while walking into the foyer. They were boisterous and happy dogs, but also well-mannered and refrained from jumping up on her.

"Hey, you hooligans! Back up and give the lady some room." A dark-haired woman with russet-brown skin who looked to be in her fifties and whose features favored Wade walked into the short hallway and gestured at the dogs.

"They're fine," Charlotte said, reaching down to the graying terrier mix that was nearest to her. "I love dogs."

"This is my mom, Maribel," Wade said to Charlotte as she straightened.

"Charlotte Halstead." She reached out to offer her hand to the woman, who grasped it and gave it a light squeeze.

"I haven't seen you since you were a tiny little thing. You and your sister."

That was right—Wade had mentioned that his mom had worked at the resort years ago. "I hope we weren't obnoxious brats," Charlotte said with a tentative smile. Was Maribel treated well when she was employed by the Halsteads? Charlotte certainly hoped so.

There had been a time, when she first went away to

college, that Charlotte was certain she wanted nothing to do with the family business and she had figured on going her own way. Then the passage of time plus basic life experience made her realize that she not only had a wonderful career opportunity right in front of her with the family business, but by being employed at the resort, she could also do some good beyond her own self-interest. She could do things for the community, like working with the literacy group she'd met with before Trey Murphy kidnapped her in her SUV. Maybe she could do things to provide for a better quality of life for resort employees, too.

"You and Dinah were sweet kids. I remember you were crazy about a collection of little toy ponies you had with a plastic corral and stables."

Charlotte hadn't thought about those little ponies in years. The memory made her smile as it brought with it thoughts of times when she and Dinah were best friends and played together all day long. *What happened? Why did things have to change?* It wasn't like they fought all the time now. They didn't really have direct conflicts. They just had such a shallow, surface relationship.

And now it was possible that she might not ever see Dinah again. They might not ever have the chance to resolve whatever it was that had pushed them apart.

"Wade and I and the rest of the Range River team are going to do everything we can to help find Dinah," Maribel said, rightly discerning the direction Charlotte's thoughts had taken at the mention of her sister's name.

Charlotte nodded. "Thank you."

"Meanwhile, welcome to the Riverside Inn." Maribel gestured toward the end of the foyer and led the way into a great room with a high ceiling sporting exposed wooden beams and a second-floor gallery with what appeared to be doors leading to bedrooms. There was a large river-stone fireplace with windows on either side that offered a view of an outside deck, the river and the mountains in the distance.

Looking around, she could see hallways, part of a kitchen and dining room, and a slight bit of what appeared to be an office or a den.

"It's beautiful," she said.

"Not as luxurious as what you're used to," Wade said beside her, "but we like it."

Charlotte cut a glance at him because there was no missing the edge to his comment. He was assuming that she'd make some kind of comparison, even if she didn't voice it, and find the inn somehow wanting. He assumed she was spoiled and critical.

Her glance lingered and he held her gaze, a hint of challenge in his eyes and a slight lift to his brows, as if throwing down a challenge and awaiting a response.

She wasn't playing this game.

She'd been born into a high-profile family—at least, high-profile in Range River—and starting somewhere around middle school, she'd encountered people who judged her and presumed things about her. About her values and how she saw herself and other people. Of course she'd wanted to fit in, wanted people to like her. And truly, despite their obsession with work and increasing the value of the family enterprise, her parents had raised Charlotte and Dinah to have respect for people who worked hard for their living, who may not have the physical comforts that the Halstead family had.

But trying to explain to people that she was not the clueless, pampered princess they assumed she was never worked. Didn't work in high school. Didn't work in college, either. She'd been tricked a few times, much to her humiliation, by people she'd thought were friends but who'd actually just wanted access to the meals and entertainments Charlotte had been able to pay for. And there had been a couple of boyfriends in college who'd eventually slipped up and exposed their true motivations for dating her—that they hoped to use Charlotte to weasel their way into the family business and get a piece of that fortune.

I'm not doing this. She broke her gaze away from Wade and shook her head slightly. She was not going to try to explain or prove herself to him. Convince him she was a decent person despite the situation she'd been born into. When she'd started attending Bible study in college, having come from a family that was nominally Christian but didn't really live in faith, she'd met the first people who weren't determined to judge her but were instead willing to accept her. And at a very dark time in her life, they'd helped her be able to accept herself.

She wasn't going to give that up just so Wade Fast Horse would accept or approve of her. Even though he was handsome in a rugged, intense kind of way. And yes, he was standing fast in support of her in a danger-ous situation, and she appreciated that. But at the end of the day, he was doing it for money. This was his *job*. And the hard lesson she'd learned still held true: she couldn't rely on anyone but herself. Getting her hopes up that Wade could somehow be different was a sure road to disappointment and heartache, yet again.

"Welcome." A man who looked maybe ten years older than Wade, about forty or so, with coffee-colored eyes and military-cut dark hair, strode out from the direction of what she could now clearly see was a cozy room furnished like a den but also housing a heavy wooden desk and several pieces of office equipment in one corner. "I'm Connor Ryan," he added.

Charlotte reached for his extended hand. "Charlotte Halstead. Thank you for letting me stay here."

"I'm hoping we can do a lot more than that and we can help you find your sister." He ushered her toward a sofa and then dropped down into a chair across from her.

Wade took a seat with Charlotte on the sofa while Maribel excused herself to resume preparing dinner.

"I'm up-to-date with everything," Connor began, with a glance at Wade. "We've got a lot going on with various cases right now, but we're going to put all the resources we can into this." Now he focused on Charlotte. "Our legitimate direction, as bounty hunters, is to go after Brett Gamble because his bond has been revoked. Wade told me he has good reason to think Gamble is involved with the disappearance of your sister and I'm inclined to agree. Since we don't have any other specific leads for Gamble, we're going to try to find him by looking for your sister."

"Thank you." Charlotte knew the police were doing everything they could to find Dinah, but having these extra hands on deck in the search—people with experiences and connections that were different from the cops and who could supplement their efforts—made her feel a little better. But not much. Charlotte tried not to dwell on the thought that her sister might not even still be alive. But that was a real possibility.

Lord, please protect her. How could so much have happened, how could her world have changed so dramatically in such a short amount of time? It was just last night that she was meeting with the literacy committee members at dinner. Thinking that afterward she would go home and catch up on a couple of episodes of her current favorite TV program.

"Charlotte?"

Charlotte's eyelids fluttered open. "Sorry." Somehow she'd nearly fallen asleep. She hadn't been able to make herself eat much of anything today and she was exhausted from everything she'd been through over the last twenty-four hours. She reached up to rub her throbbing head where she'd been struck. Apparently the ibuprofen was wearing off.

"I'll get Maribel," Connor said quietly.

"You should probably rest for a little bit," Wade said. He started to reach over and touch Charlotte's hand, but for some reason he stopped himself.

"Let's head upstairs and get you settled." Maribel walked out from the kitchen ahead of Connor. She reached for Charlotte's suitcase, but Wade was already on his feet and he beat her to it.

"I wouldn't mind a little time to wind down." Charlotte found it took more effort than she'd expected to push herself up from the couch. Her energy was draining fast.

Along with Wade and Maribel, Charlotte headed up the stairs. Then she followed as Maribel led the way along the gallery to a bedroom door at the end of the hall. She was surprised to see a longhaired tabby cat curled up on the bed.

"I'll get her out of the way," Wade said.

"No." Charlotte held up a hand to stop him. "I love cats. And I wouldn't mind some company. Who is this?"

"Her name is Fluzzy. Connor says it's because she's fluffy and fuzzy. He found her in a storm drain a couple of years ago, in pretty bad shape, so of course he had to bring her home."

The story of Fluzzy brought a smile to Charlotte's lips. She needed the reminder that even though the world was cruel at times, there was some goodness and kindness in it. Including good and kind people, she thought, as she stole a glance at Wade.

"Dinner will be ready in an hour or so," Maribel said. "I'll check with you then to see if you want to come downstairs or if you'd rather have me bring you something up here."

"I don't want to trouble you."

Maribel glanced at her son. "I'm surrounded by people who trouble me. Why should you be any different?" She smiled and winked before turning to go.

Wade lingered in the doorway. "We're going to do everything we can to find Dinah," he said. "And we'll have both you and her in our prayers."

"You're a praying person?" Charlotte asked.

He nodded. "Yes. My mom, the Ryans, they're all people of faith, too."

Charlotte felt her eyes start to tear up. "Right now, faith is the only thing getting me through all of this."

Wade nodded somberly. "Faith can do that. You keep pressing in."

With that, he stepped out and closed the door.

Charlotte stretched out on the bed. Beside her, Fluzzy opened one eye and began to rumble a low purr.

Charlotte closed her eyes, hoping to catch some sleep. And also hoping she wouldn't have nightmares about what had happened and what might be yet to come.

She had no idea what condition Dinah was in at the moment. And there was no way Charlotte could forget that she, too, was now a target for abduction. And possibly for murder.

"Charlotte's text says she'll be down here in a minute." Wade closed the message screen and slid his phone back into his pocket. "Let's give her a few minutes when she first gets down here, let her drink some coffee and maybe eat something before we spring the news on her."

A post on a local online newspaper had something to say about the Halstead family, and Charlotte in particular, that was not especially flattering and was in some ways downright alarming.

"Are you sure she doesn't already know?" Connor asked.

Wade took a sip of coffee. "She didn't mention it in her text." Although, that didn't prove anything.

He glanced over at the two men he considered brothers, Connor and Danny Ryan, who stood near him as they'd gathered by the coffeepot in the kitchen. Danny was the same age as Wade and they'd been classmates in school. While Danny's facial features resembled his older brother somewhat, the younger brother had different coloring with blue instead of brown eyes and lighter-colored hair.

Danny's wife, Tanya, had shown up alongside him at the inn this morning. While not a bounty hunter like her husband, Tanya had been in danger and needed to take refuge at the inn not so long ago. When they'd arrived, she'd told Wade and Connor that she hoped to offer comfort and reassurance to Charlotte by keeping her company at the inn as well as relating her own experience of taking refuge with the Range River Bail Bonds crew and receiving Danny's help in the middle of a dangerous and volatile situation.

The fact that Danny and Tanya had fallen in love in the midst of that ordeal and later gotten married was not lost on Wade. But he was absolutely not looking for that with Charlotte.

She seemed like a kind person, and yes, maybe there was a little bit of a spark between them. Learning that she, like him, was a person of faith had admittedly set his heart beating a little faster when she mentioned it. Because *if* he were going to set aside common sense and get married someday, his bride would have to be a believer. That was important to him.

But in reality, he didn't intend to set aside common sense. So many marriages didn't work out. So many people were, ultimately, unreliable. Some people seemed to be able to put aside those facts and give in to starry-eyed romance anyway. Wade couldn't do that. He wouldn't.

He was five years old when his dad moved out of Range River, heading to California for work. At least, that was what he'd said. His dad had also claimed he was coming back home soon. He reassured Wade on sporadic phone calls that he was just going to work a little longer, save a little more money, and then head back home to Idaho.

Wade wasn't sure when his mom had stopped believing the empty promises. Probably much sooner than the hopeful boy who didn't understand that adults sometimes lied. That *dads* sometimes lied.

His dad sent money to them for a while. But eventually the money stopped, and then the phone calls became more erratic. Finally the calls stopped, too, and his dad filed for divorce. By then his mom was working at the Wolf Lake Resort. Long hours and not much money. Their friends and neighbors, the Ryans, were going through some rough times, too, after their parents died. So the Fast Horses and the Ryans backed each other up, shared resources with each other, prayed for each other, and eventually they all found themselves working and building a future together.

Things had turned out okay. But Wade had not forgotten his own disappointment in hoping his dad would come through and do the right thing. He hadn't forgotten the heartache his mother went through or his own heartbreak after being fed promises and reassurances from his dad that were just words.

Amazingly enough, his mom wasn't bitter. He'd asked her a few times over the years if she'd ever get married again and she'd just laughed and shaken her head in response and said something along the lines of "My life is full as it is."

Wade, admittedly, was bitter. He couldn't seem to let go of the anger and resentment and the sense of being a fool when he believed his dad's promises.

No, he and Charlotte would not be falling in love like Danny and Tanya. Wade simply wasn't willing to go there. But he did like Charlotte. And he did want to help her and keep her safe. For a short while. Until the case was resolved.

Wade knew Charlotte was coming down when he heard the sound of dog toenails skittering across the wooden floor near the bottom of the stairs in the great room as the pups ran to greet her. He could hear her talking to them as she headed toward the kitchen.

"Morning," she said, rounding a corner and tucking her light hair back behind her ears.

"Good morning." Wade grabbed a mug and filled it, dumping plenty of cream and sugar into the coffee because he'd learned yesterday that that was what she liked.

While she took a couple of sips, he noted that her color was back to normal. Last night, she'd come downstairs just long enough to eat a little bit of dinner with him and Connor and Maribel. She'd looked pale then, and exhausted. She seemed more energetic now, but on the downside, a few of the light red marks that had been on the side of her face last night as a result of the kidnapping attempt had now darkened into significant bruises.

Wade introduced Charlotte to Danny and Tanya, and then everyone moved to the kitchen table, where places were set and a sausage breakfast casserole and cinnamon rolls were being kept warm in covered serving dishes.

Tanya grabbed a seat next to Charlotte, and after everyone plated their food and Maribel said grace, Tanya related her own experiences with having to be kept safe at the inn. Charlotte listened raptly and appeared to relax a little more.

Wade kept the news that he knew would disturb Charlotte to himself until everyone was finished eating. Then he realized he didn't know quite how to break it to her. She'd already been through so much, she'd gotten a small reprieve by relaxing over breakfast, and here he was, about to upset her again. He found himself stalling until Connor caught his eye and gave him a slight nod of encouragement.

Wade cleared his throat and turned to Charlotte. "So, have you looked at the local news yet today?"

She shook her head. "I haven't looked at the news, haven't read the zillions of texts people have sent me, and I definitely haven't listened to the voice mails from my parents and people calling from unfamiliar numbers. It's got to all be gossips wanting to know about Dinah's disappearance and everything that's been happening to me and I'm just not ready to deal with it all. I'll get caught up on it later." She stopped and lifted her brows. "Wait. Is there something in the news about Dinah?" She began to smile slightly. "Has she been found? Why would you make me wait until the end of breakfast to tell me?"

That dash of hopefulness in her tone made it that much worse to have to tell her the truth. "I'm sorry to say Dinah hasn't been found," he said evenly. "But what *has* happened is that someone anonymously leaked a story to the town's online newspaper that an internal auditor at the resort has discovered that *you* have been embezzling money since your return to Range River. And with Dinah missing, there's talk that she may have been involved in stealing money, as well."

Wade stopped talking and waited. His job often involved confronting people with the facts of unlawful things they'd done. If she immediately came up with an excuse or a belabored explanation, that would tell him what he needed to know. That she was guilty. Even if she didn't directly confess.

He steeled himself for the burn of disappointment if

it turned out he'd misread her. That, like his dad, she'd been taking advantage of his trust.

Instead, she laughed. For kind of a long time, like she was either releasing stress or building up anxiety to a breaking point. Wade had no idea where it was going. Until she finally stopped, took a deep breath, shook her head and said, "You can't be serious."

"I am."

She crossed her arms, sat back in her chair and said, "Well, I didn't steal anything. The timing of this is bizarre. Maybe it's not coincidental that it's happening while Dinah is missing." She shook her head. "Once again, I have *no idea* what is going on. But I do know it's possible to hire someone to do a forensic computer audit and discover who actually played around with the accounts. If I have to pay for someone to do that and prove my innocence, I will."

"So you didn't do it?" Wade asked, encouraged by her confidence that her name would be cleared. "You didn't pilfer any money?"

"I did not. And if you don't believe me, I'll thank you for your hospitality and I'll leave."

"Not so fast." Connor held up a hand. "Just because we want to talk to you about this doesn't mean we're accusing you of actually doing it. But we had to ask. You must understand that."

Charlotte gave a sharp nod.

"We have a bounty hunting aspect to our business because we want to get dangerous fugitives off the streets," Connor continued. "But it's only part of our bigger bail bond business. We write bail bonds because the law presumes people are innocent until proven guilty. If bail is set, then arrestees have the right to post bail and walk free unless or until circumstances change. Being in this business for a few years, I've learned the innocent people do sometimes get arrested and charged. Their reputations are smeared and they're embarrassed. Sometimes their future careers are imperiled over something they didn't even do because news stories seem to live online forever and corrections and updates clearing a person's name aren't always issued."

Charlotte smiled faintly and sighed deeply. After a moment, she glanced at Wade.

"You say you didn't do it and I believe you." The words were out of Wade's mouth before he realized it. But what he said was true. His common sense might be inclined to remind him that he barely knew her. But some other part of him had come to the conclusion that she was the honorable woman that she appeared to be.

For reasons he didn't want to think about, that realization troubled him.

"Our sister, Hayley, and her husband, Jack, are tied up with a manhunt for Eagle Rapids Bail Bonds right now." Connor fixed his gaze on Charlotte. "Danny and I also have other cases we're working, but we'll still be able to put out the word to our own confidential informants in town and see what we can learn about Gamble and Murphy and anything else related to your sister."

"Thank you." Charlotte nodded. "I'll look into this embezzlement issue on my own."

"Jonah and Lorraine can do some deeper research on Gamble and Murphy and see if they can learn anything useful," Maribel suggested. The trusted office assistants were often helpful in gathering background information. "Also, I believe Jonah's got connections at the online newspaper. He may be able to learn how the embezzlement story was delivered to the journalist there who posted it. Maybe we can find out who is feeding the lies and get some kind of lead from that."

"Good idea." Connor set his empty coffee cup on the table. He turned to Wade. "What do you have planned for today?"

"I figured we'd visit the coffee shop that Dinah manages on the resort property. Talk to the employees. See if anything unusual has been happening there lately. If anyone suspicious has been coming around. If Dinah seemed worried or fearful."

"That sounds reasonable." Charlotte set her napkin on the table and stood, a determined expression on her face. She picked up her plate and utensils to clear her spot at the table. "But before we go to the coffee shop, I intend to find my parents and talk to them face-to-face about this embezzlement issue." She shook her head. "I haven't done anything wrong and I'm not going to hide from this."

Wade watched her stride over to the kitchen to put her dishes in the dishwasher. Not exactly the type of behavior he'd expect from the daughter of wealthy resort owners. He'd assumed she was used to people cleaning up after her.

Beyond pondering that, he couldn't help worrying about her safety. Leaving the inn and going back into town could make her a target yet again. But the truth was he could benefit from her assistance in getting information that might help find her sister as well as his bail jumper.

Charlotte was willing to take a risk to do what she felt had to be done: find her sister and clear her own name. Wade was determined to do his best to protect her while she did that.

SIX

"I don't think it's a good time for you to go in right now." Arthur Halstead's personal secretary stood behind her desk, apparently thinking her positioning might slow Charlotte down.

"Don't worry, Stella. I'll shoulder the blame for barging in." Charlotte continued past her, with Wade close on her heels, and shoved open the heavy wooden double door leading into her father's office. Thanks to Stella, she already knew her mother was in there with him. But she was surprised to see a third person there, as well.

"Mr. Deming." Charlotte managed to hide her surprise and gave the man a nod of greeting.

"Ms. Halstead." He smiled in return. Though the smile didn't appear to reach his eyes, which were cold and assessing.

Nolan Deming represented an investment group out of Dallas that had been trying to outright purchase the resort, or at least purchase a percentage of it, for years. Her parents were adamant that they would never sell, but they took meetings with Deming once or twice a year because in return he sent business their way in the form of several large conferences run by Texans excited to get out of the Dallas heat in the summer and cool off beside a mountain lake.

Charlotte's parents—both appearing pale and worried, as would be expected since one of their daughters was missing—got to their feet and each of them gave her a weary hug. But, as was so often the case, it seemed to be mostly for show. She could tell they were annoyed by her interruption. Especially after she told them she wasn't there to give them news on the search for Dinah.

She told herself that her parents were themselves upset and traumatized by Dinah's disappearance and that it was unfair of her to expect a warmer reaction from them.

Still, she was disappointed. And a little sad.

She made a brief introduction between Wade and Deming, whose eyes widened when he heard the term *bounty hunter*. At the same moment, Kandace made a slight scoffing sound. Charlotte heard it but she didn't care whether her mother approved of Wade or not. Let her mom have whatever opinion she wanted. The man had already helped Charlotte escape potentially lethal situations, twice. And yes, he was getting paid to hunt down the bad guys. But he'd already offered her and the Halstead family help and support beyond what could have been reasonably expected by a man just doing his job.

"Honey, why don't the three of us talk later." Her mom gave her a pointed look.

Of course her parents would want to keep a shiny gloss on things as much as possible. That was their default attitude on everything related to the Halstead public profile and the family business. And Charlotte agreed that there were plenty of situations that a family should keep private and quiet. But right now, when it came to Dinah's disappearance and the charges of business impropriety publicly leveled against Charlotte, they were way beyond that point.

"Mom, the story that I pilfered money from the resort has been published in an *online newspaper*. It's out there, whether we like it or not. And I want to make an equally public statement that I haven't taken anything. The story is an outright lie and I intend to find out who reported it. Meanwhile, tell me right now—do you believe you have actual evidence that I embezzled money?"

"That's enough!" Arthur Halstead's complexion had gone from pale to beet red. He was furious. After making eye contact with Charlotte, he glanced at Nolan Deming—who appeared enthralled by the drama unfolding in front of him—and then back at Charlotte again. The message was crystal clear: this shameful situation needed to be kept hidden and discussed out of earshot of witnesses.

"I don't have anything to hide," Charlotte said. Despite the feeling of heat in her cheeks and the increasing pounding of her heart, she fought to keep her voice calm. "Along with trying to find my missing sister and keep from getting *killed*, I now need to deal with this? Okay, I want to deal with it, head-on. I want to fight it. *Publicly*, because the accusation has been made public.

"And who knows?" she continued. "Maybe this fabricated story is related to Dinah's disappearance and the attacks on me. You know, Dad, there was another attack on me yesterday and it wasn't a case of those jerks Murphy and Gamble mistaking me for Dinah for a second time." Despite her best efforts, Charlotte found herself choking up, and tears of heartbreak and frustration pooled in the corners of her eyes. "Those criminals made it clear they knew who I was and that they were after *me*, personally."

"I'm sorry that happened to you," her father said, while her mother nodded in agreement.

She used the backs of her hands to impatiently wipe away the tears that were now rolling down her cheeks as a feeling of emptiness and abandonment hollowed out her chest. Some part of her had hoped for a more emotional response from her parents. Some words of warmth and expression of their faith in her. *Something* other than a response that made it clear their focus was more strongly on their business.

But really, what had she been thinking, expecting something like that? As her parents continued to simply look at her with sympathetic expressions, and Nolan Deming had a slight smile on his face—whether it was embarrassment or something else, she couldn't tell— Charlotte realized that this was how they were and they weren't going to change. And her thoughts flickered to Dinah, as she wondered how much her alienation from her twin had come from Dinah's decision to make their parents happy by hiding her *unappealing* emotions and just stamping down those feelings however she could.

Like with drugs, or alcohol, or compulsive spending.

Or in Charlotte's case, she'd dealt with them by doubting herself, being afraid to say how she truly felt, and ultimately running away to Seattle as soon as she could. All things she did before faith took root in her heart and she realized she truly was a cherished child of God. No matter what anyone else said or implied. And that had made her all the stronger.

The awkwardness of the moment began to sink in and Charlotte felt physically deflated. Almost like she could collapse. But Wade, who'd remained quiet for the last few moments, stepped closer to her side. While he didn't actually reach over to touch her, she could feel his presence nevertheless. And when she turned to him, the warmth and encouragement she saw in his eyes refilled her with confidence. Remembering their conversation about faith, she offered up a quick prayer and petition for support. *My help comes from the Lord, maker of heaven and earth.*

"If any evidence shows up that appears to prove I pilfered money from the resort, will you forward that to me?" Charlotte asked, shifting her gaze between both her parents.

"Yes," her father said tightly. When he didn't add anything further, and her mother didn't chime in with any kind of reassurance, Charlotte realized she'd been dismissed. There was nothing to be gained by staying.

"Let's go," she said to Wade.

"I'm with you."

As they both turned, he moved his hand slightly toward hers, brushing her fingers. He didn't take hold, but his touch was intentional, lasting longer than it would have if it had happened by accident. In that moment, when Charlotte was feeling so alone, it was nearly as powerful as a hug. It was a feeling that she'd craved for much of her life. A sense that someone understood what she was feeling and was offering their support. Even in an ugly situation. Maybe at a moment when she wasn't behaving as her best self.

Wade opened the door, and as Charlotte stepped past him and into the anteroom where Stella was stationed just outside the office, she was finally able to muster up a faint smile for him to express her appreciation. Instead of smiling back, the bounty hunter raised his eyebrows and shook his head slightly as if in disbelief. "That was rough," he said quietly.

Finally, someone understood that things were not always as rosy and enviable with the Halstead family as they appeared to be. *Wade* understood.

Or maybe he was just pretending to understand. Because he had a job to do and it would be easier for him if he got along with Charlotte. Like the resort staff had pretended to care about her because it was part of their job.

She sighed as fears and worries from her past came flooding back, and she fought to remind herself that right now she needed to focus on her missing sister and not on herself.

"Charlotte!" Ethan, looking haggard with dark circles under his eyes and uncharacteristic stubble visible on his chin and cheeks, rushed toward her and wrapped his arms around her in a tight embrace. "I heard you were in the building and I came to see for myself that you were okay."

He finally released her, his gaze appearing to linger on the bruises on her face that she'd tried to cover with makeup. Meanwhile, she took in the sight of him. While he might seem to have a reasonable appearance to anyone who didn't know him, Charlotte could see the toll Dinah's disappearance had taken on her boyfriend. Normally, Ethan was clean-shaven and sharply dressed with every hair in place. At the moment, he looked like he might have slept in his suit, and his tie was slightly askew.

"Any word on Dinah?" he quickly asked.

Charlotte shook her head. "No. And I assume you already know that the police haven't offered an update beyond the assurance that they're still searching for her."

"Yes. I heard about the attack on you yesterday. It showed up on the police blotter of the online newspaper. Man, you've been through a lot."

"I've got a bodyguard alongside me." She smiled and gestured at Wade, attempting to lighten the mood a little.

Ethan and Wade exchanged nods.

"So," Ethan began, dragging out the word. "Have you seen the *other* news about you? Besides the attack yesterday?"

"You mean the anonymous report that I embezzled money? Yes, I've seen it. And it's a lie. I haven't taken anything. As a matter of fact, you could help me clear my name. Do you have any idea what the specific supposed evidence against me might be?" As the operations manager, he would be involved in investigating the claim.

"We're still looking into that. The newspaper refused to tell us who contacted them with the information or to show us specifically what evidence they had. If any. Actually, if you read the article closely, you'll see lots of terms like *reported* and *alleged*, which makes me wonder if they ran with a weak story just for the sake of a sensationalistic headline and getting people to click on the article while at the same time avoiding a potential libel lawsuit." He drew in a deep sigh. "We're doing an emergency audit right now." He winced. "And I'm sorry, but on your parents' orders, we retrieved your work laptop from your condo and we've got a tech taking a look at it."

"Well, they won't find anything damaging on that," Charlotte said firmly.

"Do you have any theories on why this accusation would come so close on the heels of Dinah's disappearance?" Wade asked.

Ethan shook his head. "I don't have any theories on *anything*. One minute life is going along like normal, and the next minute it feels like the whole world has gone off the rails."

Charlotte and Wade walked with Ethan back to his office, and then continued to the elevator for the trip down to the resort's ground floor. On the way, Charlotte filled Wade in on Nolan Deming and his company's yearslong attempt to purchase an interest in the resort or even the whole property outright. She also gave him a quick summary of Ethan's history with the Wolf Lake Resort and with Dinah in particular.

"Do you think there's a connection between this Deming guy showing up and the attacks on you and Dinah?" Wade asked as they reached the bottom floor.

Startled by the idea, Charlotte turned to him. "How so?"

He shrugged. "I don't know. I just find it pays to keep track of random bits of information and maintain an open mind about how those pieces might fit together. I don't have a specific theory or anything, I'm just thinking out loud."

Charlotte puzzled over the various *random bits of information*, as Wade called them. There was Dinah and her drug and alcohol issues. Gamble's claim Dinah owed him something. Money, presumably. And Wade's suggestion that Deming making a visit right now might somehow be connected to the kidnapping attempts.

"Ready to go talk to Dinah's coworkers at the resort's coffee shop?" Wade asked as the elevator doors opened and they stepped onto the highly polished lobby floors.

Charlotte nodded. The coffee shop was located in its own separate building on resort property beside the street so it could take advantage of drive-through customers. Wade had already mentioned the need to be extremely vigilant once they stepped outside, reminding her that she was a vulnerable target.

As they walked through the lobby toward the exit, Charlotte couldn't help noticing that staff members who were normally friendly were now avoiding eye contact with her. As with any workplace, the rumor mill at the resort was fast-moving. For a moment it seemed she could feel their suspicion, but then she shook it off. In the scheme of things, what difference did their opinion make?

What really mattered was finding Dinah, as soon as possible, alive and well. Charlotte willed herself to think only in those terms, that her twin was still alive and in decent shape. So many stories were told of twins *knowing* when one another was in trouble. Knowing if the other was alive or dead. Charlotte had no such sense when it came to her own identical twin. Which made the current situation all the sadder.

"Charlotte!"

For the second time this morning, she heard someone call out her name. This time it was a female voice, and she turned to see a woman waving her hand and hurrying toward her. Charlotte kept going.

"Who is that?" Wade asked.

"My cousin Kim Halstead Riggs."

"Aren't you going to stop and talk to her?"

"I suppose I have to." Charlotte made herself stop and offer the friendliest greeting she could muster given the stressful conditions of what her life had become over the last few days.

Her cousin took a long, lingering, head-to-toe look at Wade before turning to Charlotte and smiling expectantly. Charlotte made the introductions. Wade was impressively polite with the rude woman.

"I'm sorry, but we really don't have time to chat right now," Charlotte said before Kim could ask the questions she appeared to be dying to put forth. "We're doing our best to find Dinah and we've got to get going. I'm sure you understand."

"Of course," her cousin responded, appearing slightly put off. "I just wanted to offer my condolences."

"No one's dead," Charlotte snapped. And then immediately regretted her tone.

"Of course not. I'm sorry. Bad choice of words. But do let me know if there's any way I can help."

"I will. Thank you. Now, please excuse us." Charlotte turned and resumed walking. Wade stayed by her side.

"I take it you and your cousin aren't particularly close?"

Charlotte blew out a deep breath. "Oh, Kim drives me crazy with her drama and I just don't have time for it. Her dad inherited an interest in the resort and he sold it to my dad as soon as he turned twenty-one. He blew through all the money and Kim never stops lamenting that she should by rights still have a financial stake in the resort. That it's clearly what our great-grandfather who started the business would have wanted."

"Huh. So do you think she figures that if something

happened to you and your sister, then after your parents are gone she'd inherit the resort?"

Charlotte sighed. "I know you want to consider every angle, just like the cops do, but I really think that's pushing it. Kim is annoying, but she's not deadly. Besides, once my parents are gone and Dinah and I have the property, we'll help Kim out with a little something extra financially. We've talked about it. My parents aren't willing to do that, but I say, why not? We don't have a very big family. Why shouldn't we share some of what we have? Plus, Kim has been working here for most of her life."

"Are there any people here that you *do* get along with?" Wade asked just before they stepped outside.

Charlotte turned to him. He offered her a teasing grin.

"There's tension between you and your parents, you and your sister, and you and your cousin," he continued. "Seems to me you must be kind of touchy."

"What do you think?" she asked. And she was serious. Because she did have a lot of tension with her family and maybe it really was her fault and she didn't realize it. She felt like Wade would tell her the truth.

"I don't know any of you well enough to have an opinion," he responded. "But maybe, after all of this is resolved, you could put a little more effort into understanding it all a little better. And maybe letting go of a few old grudges if you need to."

Her first instinct was to defend herself. But she'd asked his opinion, so she thought about it for a moment and then finally nodded. Ultimately, it was probably a fair response.

They stepped outside and immediately she felt her

whole body tense. Especially when she saw Wade looking in every direction, head on a swivel and hand over the pistol she knew was tucked in a holster under his jacket. Her sister's life was in danger. Her own life was in danger. And, just by walking beside him, she was putting Wade's life in danger, too.

Please, Lord, let Dinah be okay and let us both live through this. Please don't end either of our lives before we have a chance to revive the love and closeness we had when we were children.

"Dinah would typically pop in and out of the shop several times a day. Occasionally, she'd give a reason for leaving. Like saying she had a hair appointment. But most of the time she'd just say she was stepping out for a while." The coffee shop's assistant manager offered Wade and Charlotte a slight shrug.

Wade nodded encouragingly, hoping the young woman would keep talking and add a few helpful details. Instead, the manager, who'd stepped away from the busy counter to talk to them, simply looked at him. She'd expressed her concern for Dinah to Charlotte the moment they'd walked into the shop, and assured her she wanted to do everything she could to help Dinah get rescued.

Wade took a quick glance around the interior of the coffee shop. It was almost completely glass on three sides, offering beautiful views of the surrounding park, a section of the main resort building, a strip of Wolf Lake and the snow-dotted mountain peaks jutting skyward not too far away. It might make for a picturesque setting to sit and sip coffee, but with Gamble and Murphy intent on harming Charlotte for reasons that were still unknown, he didn't want to remain here very long. It would be too easy for anyone stalking her to get a clear view through the windows and fire an accurate shot. While prior efforts had been directed at kidnapping her, there was no telling when the situation might escalate to an intentionally lethal attack.

"It looks like business is good," Charlotte commented to the manager.

There were several patrons standing in line and sitting at tables.

The young woman nodded. "We stay pretty busy."

As they spoke, Wade again scanned the three window walls to keep an eye out for threats.

"We're obviously here because we're hoping to get a lead on finding my sister," Charlotte continued. "Maybe you could give us a little more help. Did you notice anything unusual going on around here? Or *anyone* unusual? Perhaps someone that seemed to make Dinah nervous?"

The manager shook her head. "Can't say that I have. Like I mentioned, she wasn't around all the time. Apparently she had other things going on that she thought were more important."

Wade heard the hint of disapproval in the assistant manager's voice. It sounded like she took her job seriously but her boss, daughter of the coffee shop's owners, did not.

"I'm going to be blunt because we can't afford to waste time," Charlotte said. "Do you have any ideas on what's going on? Any theories on who might be angry enough with my sister to endanger her? Thoughts on why she might owe money to a criminal?"

The manager's eyes widened on the phrase *owe money to a criminal*. "I show up every workday and do my job. And part of my boss's job." She gave Charlotte a meaningful look. "I stay busy. I mind my own business. I go home. That's it." She paused for a moment. "I vaguely remember a guy coming by and asking for her a couple of times. He didn't want to leave his name or tell me what it was regarding. I think he had brown hair. There wasn't anything particularly distinctive about him, and it wasn't like he seemed threatening or anything, so he didn't make that much of an impression." She shook her head. "Beyond that, I can't think of anything that could help you."

"That was disappointing," Charlotte said as she and Wade stepped out of the coffee shop a few minutes later.

He nodded. "Welcome to bounty hunting. Dead ends. Unanswered questions. People who don't know anything about your case, or at least won't *tell* you anything about it. Like Stuart at Club Sapphire. But if you keep at it, doggedly, eventually something turns up."

Well, one hoped and prayed that eventually something turned up. Some fugitives went missing for a very long time. Some cases had been open so long that it was only reasonable to assume that the fugitive had passed on without being found. But Wade didn't want to mention that reality right now. Not when Charlotte appeared so discouraged. Nevertheless, there genuinely was reason for them to hope that they would find her sister and Wade's bail jumper.

Crack!

"Gun!" Wade threw his body atop Charlotte's, sending them both tumbling to the ground outside the front of the coffee shop. Shredded glass flew in all directions as three more shots quickly followed.

He and Charlotte were partially hidden behind a bistro table and chair they'd knocked over on their way to the ground, but the table was lightweight and Wade knew it wouldn't offer much protection from bullets. Making the situation more worrisome, he could tell by the sound of the shots that the shooter was using a rifle, which would give the assailant better accuracy. Staying put, hunkering down and hoping for the best was not a good option.

"Are you hit?" Wade asked, still shielding Charlotte with his body.

"No. Are you?" Her voice was shaky.

Pressed so close to her, Wade could feel her pulse pounding in fear. "I'm okay." For her sake, he tried to sound calm even though he felt anything but that.

Screams and sounds of chaos spilled out from the coffee shop.

For the sake of their own safety, as well as the people inside the coffee shop, Wade and Charlotte needed to move to a better location as quickly as possible.

After a few beats of silence, Wade rose up slightly and crawled forward to peer around the tabletop. He looked in the direction the gunshot sounds had come from, but didn't see anyone. He assumed that Gamble and Murphy had come after Charlotte again and they'd changed their tactics. As Wade feared, they'd escalated from kidnapping to an outright attempt at murder.

Were the two perps working side by side? Or had they spread out, each of them targeting Charlotte and him from a different position and making it more difficult for them to take cover?

Lord, please help me know what to do.

He took a quick look around. They were too far from the main resort building to attempt a sprint in that direction. Going back into the coffee shop would be like walking into a trap. The shooters could follow them in there and finish the hit. Staying in position would get them killed. They *had* to move. And right now the best option was to race around to the back of the coffee shop, where they would at least have the concrete wall protecting their backs. Maybe get behind a metal trash bin and hunker down there until the cops showed up. Someone must have called them by now.

He did have his gun. But escalating the situation into an outright gun battle with Charlotte and so many other innocent people around was the last thing he wanted to do.

"We need to move." Wade took a deep breath. Staying crouched, he managed to get his feet underneath him and help Charlotte to do the same.

A volley of three more shots tore across the edge of the table they'd been hiding behind, the bullets pinging loudly and sending it wobbling before blasting into the window behind their intended targets.

"That was close," Charlotte said.

"Yeah. Their aim is getting more accurate. We've got to go."

"Where to?"

"We'll run to the back. There's got to be a large trash can or something we can hide behind." He drew his gun, hoping he wouldn't have to use it.

"You go first. I'll be right behind you." He intended to place his body between Charlotte and the shooters. "They'll expect us to stay pinned down. We've got an element of surprise by making a move, but we've got to use it aggressively. When I give the word, I want you to dart up and run around to the back of the building as fast as you can. Okay?"

She drew a deep breath, turned to him, her eyes wide with fear, and nodded.

"Okay," he said. *"Go!"*

They both took off running, away from the direction of the shooter and around the building to the back.

There was a delay of a few seconds before Wade heard shots fired. The tactic of taking the shooter by surprise when he and Charlotte broke cover and ran had evidently worked.

As he'd hoped, there was a large commercial trash can on a cement slab at the back of the shop. They dived behind it, curling up until they were completely hidden.

"At least Dinah's employees keep the area back here swept clean," Charlotte muttered. Her voice was still shaky. For good reason—she was still terrified. But she was trying to stay strong and Wade admired her for it. While getting shot at wasn't an everyday occurrence for him, he did have extensive training for dealing with violent situations. Charlotte did not.

Crack! The rifle shots began again, the bullet strikes making dull metallic thunking sounds as they struck the thick steel oversize trash can.

Wade's plan hadn't worked for long. *Where are the police?*

He peered around the corner, hoping to see which of the thugs was shooting at them and get a fix on exactly where the assailant was located. He saw movement between two parked cars, someone crouched down, but partially visible through the car windows.

And then, to Wade's surprise, the shooter moved around the car and headed straight toward him. To his greater surprise, the would-be assassin was neither of the two goons he and Charlotte had been dealing with up to this event. He'd seen the man before, but he couldn't think when or where.

Right now it didn't matter. The gunman was moving in for the kill and Wade had to take control of the situation. "Stay here," he said to Charlotte. Ignoring her protests, he moved away from their hiding place and ran for the row of parked cars on the edge of the street. His plan was to try to get behind the shooter and get him to give up and drop his weapon.

The shooter fired a couple of rounds at him, but Wade moved quickly in a zigzag pattern and managed to evade the shots. Crouched between two parked cars, he could see the industrial trash can that was shielding Charlotte and he could see the shooter. Staying bent down, he raced along the row of parked cars and was nearly at the point when he could attack the assailant from behind when the gunman began to run toward Charlotte's hiding place.

Wade raced toward him. "Stop! I'll shoot!"

The rifleman spun and fired at him before moving again.

Wade dropped to the ground. The slight hill now directly behind the assailant would prevent any bullets from striking an innocent bystander. Wade fired three rounds.

The attacker spun around and once again headed for cover behind the parked cars.

Seconds later, Wade heard the sound of a motorcycle engine growling to life in the direction where the shooter had disappeared. And then it sped away.

SEVEN

"The shooter was a professional *hit man*?" Charlotte could barely speak the words. An hour had passed since the assailant disappeared. She was now sitting with Wade in the living room of her condo on the resort grounds as they were being interviewed by Detective Romanov. A couple of patrons had been cut by broken glass, but otherwise no one else in the coffee shop had been injured.

Fear and anxiety still held a tight grip on Charlotte's lungs. She was trembling—more so now than during the attack—as adrenaline swirled through her body, making her jittery and light-headed at the same time.

"I'm afraid so." Wade exchanged glances with the detective before turning back to Charlotte. "It took me a little while to realize why he looked familiar. His name is Paul Boutin. He skipped on a substantial bail bond a little over a year ago. Range River Bail Bonds didn't write his bond, but as a bounty hunter, I can still go after him."

"Who would want to *hire* someone to kill me?" Charlotte said softly, looking down at her feet and shaking her head. "And why?"

"Let's talk about that for a minute," Romanov said.

Charlotte and Wade had already given their statements on the specific actions that had happened at the coffee shop, both to the initial responding officers and to the detective.

"It's been over twenty-four hours since your sister was discovered missing, and in that time you've almost been abducted for a second time and now you're the target of a contracted hit. We haven't received a ransom demand for your sister, which is something I expected."

Charlotte gave in to a sob that she'd been struggling to hold back. She couldn't help it. That turned into a couple of minutes of her crying while repeatedly trying to collect herself, but her emotions were too far out of her control. She was scared for her sister, scared for herself, bewildered by what was going on and frightened by thoughts of what might happen next.

Beyond that, coming back here to her condo to talk to the detective, where she'd thought the familiar surroundings would give her a feeling of normalcy and strength, had been a mistake. As soon as she'd stepped through the door, being back here had triggered horrible memories of how she'd felt the moment she realized her twin was missing and that something was terribly wrong.

Romanov waited patiently.

Wade spotted a box of tissues on an end table, walked over to get it, and then held it out toward Charlotte.

"Thank you." She grabbed a few tissues and began to dab at her eyes and wipe her nose.

After a moment's hesitation, Wade sat down on the sofa beside her and wrapped his arm around her shoulders.

Charlotte leaned into him, allowing herself to take momentary comfort in the warmth and strength he offered while warning herself not to think his gesture meant anything. Or that the support he offered was something that would last. So many times in her life when she'd been sad or upset about something and leaned on someone—typically one of her parents, and later, her twin sister—they'd quickly withdrawn. Maybe they hadn't wanted to share her burden. Or maybe they hadn't wanted to feel that closely connected to her. Either way, the sorrowful ache from the resulting feeling of abandonment had left her feeling worse than before.

She couldn't stand to have that feeling after letting herself depend too much on Wade.

She had to depend on *herself.* She had to be strong on her own. And through pressing into her faith. The idea that unwavering support could exist in the world around her was just an illusion. Something that people pretended. Just as her family pretended to be warm and close and cuddly for the sake of resort promotional photos back when she was a kid and a teenager.

Charlotte made herself push away from Wade's embrace even though she didn't really want to. It would be better, in the long run, to remember that he was a bounty hunter getting paid to do a job. Like the resort staff members around her when she was growing up. He was not actually her friend.

"We've got detectives and patrol officers covering varied aspects of this case," Romanov finally said, getting her interview back on track. "Surveillance video, credit card trails, phone records, all kinds of potential sources to develop leads. But right now I'd like to approach things from a different perspective and take a look at the possible motivation behind all of this. Specifically, money as a motivation. Do you have any theories?"

"Maybe Dinah has some kind of drug debt." Charlotte shook her head. "That's the only thing I can think of."

"There's a Halstead cousin who may ultimately have a claim to the resort property if something were to happen to Charlotte and Dinah," Wade interjected.

Charlotte laughed dismissively. She couldn't help it. "Kim? You think *Kim* is somehow involved." She shook her head at the ridiculousness of his suggestion.

"I think you might be so used to the wealth you grew up with that you don't realize the lengths many people would go to just to have a piece of it," Wade said grimly.

Ah, yes. Here it was again. The reminder that she'd grown up in a family with money and stature and therefore everything must have been perfectly smooth sailing for her. She couldn't possibly have any sense of what life was like for anyone else.

She itched to tell him a little bit more about herself. The lessons she'd learned both growing up here at the resort and when she went away to college. She'd experienced a lot of things in Seattle that were new to her. She'd learned some hard lessons about herself. She'd also come to understand, through her faith walk and by volunteering her time with people in dire circumstances, that people made mistakes and deserved to be forgiven. And that she needed to be a forgiver herself.

But explaining to people that she wasn't the kind of person they'd presumed her to be felt like she was begging for their approval. Her sense of self-respect had finally demanded that she stop doing that. In the end, people generally didn't want to believe her, anyway.

Changing preconceived notions demanded too much effort.

"There's also a man in town named Nolan Deming you might want to check out," Wade said to Romanov. "He represents an investment group that's looking to purchase the resort. Or at least an interest in it. I don't know if that could somehow lead to an attack on the Halstead twins, but it seems worth a look."

This time, Charlotte couldn't laugh at his comment. Absurd as it seemed, maybe he was right. Maybe these larger-than-life plots were more realistic than she'd realized. Maybe, because she'd never been desperate for money, she didn't really understand what other people might do to get it. Or to get *more* of it. Even people she knew. Or thought she knew.

"Did you want to tell me anything about the embezzlement claims?" the detective asked.

Of course Romanov would know about that. Charlotte blew out a sigh.

"It's a complete fabrication," Charlotte replied, looking directly at the cop. "Take me down to the station and give me a lie detector test, if you want to. The *anonymous rumor* in the town's online newspaper has no validity whatsoever. Maybe it's related to all this other stuff that's going on. It could just be someone wanting to kick me while I'm down." She shook her head. "I'm angry and insulted about it. But right now I'm much more focused on finding my sister. And on keeping myself alive."

Sad and scary that she had to add that last bit, but it was true. Suddenly it was a fight just for her to make it through the day without some assailant trying to harm her. But she was not going to back down from the challenge.

"Okay." Romanov got to her feet. "This gives me enough to think about for now."

Charlotte and Wade also stood.

"I don't know if you were planning to move back home." The detective glanced around the condo. "But I suggest you continue to stay with Wade and the rest of his team at the inn. At least for now."

"Agreed," Wade said.

"Thank you." Charlotte let a glance flicker in his direction, but she didn't allow it to linger. She didn't need a reminder that the face she'd originally thought looked so harsh now appeared compassionate and handsome to her. And she definitely didn't want to dwell on how comforting it had felt for his arm to be wrapped around her.

There was enough danger coming at her from violent criminals—including paid assassins, apparently. It would be foolish to put her heart in danger, too. And it would be dangerous for her to care too much about Wade.

"Let me take you back to the inn so you can get some rest. You've been through a lot." Wade continually looked around while he spoke, hyperaware that there was a hit man at large who'd apparently been hired to take out Charlotte. Police were still on the resort property, a couple of them within view as he and Charlotte made their way to his truck, but that didn't mean she was safe. A skilled marksman could hit a target from very far away. And the shooter obviously took care to make sure he had a solid escape plan.

"What exactly are you going to do after you get rid of me?" Charlotte asked once they were in the truck and headed down the road.

"I'm not *getting rid* of you." He tried an amused tone to lighten the mood, but it didn't work. When he glanced over, she was looking at him with drawn brows and her arms tightly crossed at her chest. "I want you safe," he continued. "It was probably a mistake to let you work alongside me, anyway."

There was no *probably*. He was certain, now, that it had been a mistake.

"I want me to be safe, too."

From the corner of his eye, Wade could see her un-cross her arms before she continued.

"*Believe* me. I've had nightmares about *both* attempts at kidnapping me. And the back of my head still hurts from getting smacked outside the diner." She reached up to touch it. "After this is over, I hope I never take safety and security for granted again. Ever. But we both know it isn't over yet. And I still believe I can help."

"Yeah, about that…" Wade could be diplomatic when he wanted to be. Especially in the pursuit of a fugitive, when finesse and manipulation were often required to get answers quickly from a reluctant witness. When it came to his personal life, he preferred being direct and honest. And he liked it when people were that way with him. He'd choose being insulted or having his feelings hurt over having someone hide what they were truly thinking any day. He supposed he could thank his un-reliable dad for that.

"You haven't been able to get people to open up and give us information about Dinah like we thought you would," he finally said after a few moments of silence. "Turns out that tactic isn't paying off and it's too slow. Romanov did mention that the cops were contacting Dinah's friends. Maybe the intimidation factor of cops asking her associates questions might prove to have a better payoff than your influence due to being her sister. Or being the friend or acquaintance of the person being questioned. Or even being one of the famous Halstead twins."

"Famous Halstead twins?"

The anger in her words shocked him. "Well, you are a Halstead and your family is regionally well-known." Why was she overreacting? Was it because of a couple of the comments he'd made? About her family, their business, their status? But what he'd said was true. Or maybe it wasn't. He didn't know her. Not really.

But he'd like to.

"Look, I'm sorry—"

"Don't," she interrupted him. While she'd sounded angry before, now she sounded tired.

She'd been through so much, was still going through so much. And he'd been a jerk. Didn't matter that he hadn't realized the apparent depth of the sting of his words at the time he'd said them, that was no excuse. He knew better. And he didn't even want to think about how stressed and touchy and out of sorts he'd feel if Hayley or Danny or Connor Ryan were missing.

He wanted to apologize, but she'd just told him not to.

"I didn't think—"

"Let's focus on Dinah," she said, interrupting him

again. "I have an idea, but first, tell me what you plan to do after taking me back to the inn."

"I intend to visit a few of my informants. Wave a little cash in front of them as incentive and see if I can motivate them to work harder to get information on Gamble and Murphy and, now, the hit man Paul Boutin. Get them to put their ear to the ground and find out what people are saying about your sister. I plan to get Hayley and the guys to press their informants harder, too. And my brother-in-law, Jack, and the bounty hunters at his bail bonds agency."

He glanced over and she gave him a tight nod. "That sounds like a good plan."

"So, how do you think you can help?"

"Turn right up here," she said as they approached an intersection near the center of town, "and I'll tell you."

Intrigued, Wade made the turn. He glanced in the rearview mirror to see if anyone turned behind them. He'd been watching to see if they were being tailed since they left the resort. So far, it looked as if they were in the clear.

"Slow down," Charlotte said after they'd gone a short distance. And then she directed him to park in front of a bohemian-looking shop with wind chimes hanging from the eaves in front of it. Flowers were painted on the window and there was a ceramic horse painted with a paisley pattern stationed by the front door.

"What's this?" Wade hadn't noticed the business before.

"I guess it's my last shot at trying to get information about Dinah from someone unexpected. Someone she's known for a long time. Maybe a confidante of sorts."

Continuing to keep an eye on their surroundings as they got out of the truck, Wade followed Charlotte toward the door, where he saw that the establishment was a hair salon. "Seriously?" he said as he pulled open the door and ushered Charlotte in ahead of him.

The place was busy. But it looked like a typical hair salon his mom or Hayley would go to, from what Wade could see. Not like a place that wealthy and stylish Dinah Halstead would patronize.

"Janelle and Dinah and I go way back," Charlotte said. "Although, she was really more of Dinah's friend than mine back when we were in high school. By the time Dinah quit college and moved back home, Janelle had opened this shop. Dinah originally came here just to visit an old friend. But she liked Janelle's work and kept coming back." Charlotte glanced around at the potted plants and eye-catching mixture of original artwork and photographs of exotic locations hanging on the walls. Then she drew in a deep breath through her nose. Wade had already noticed the scented candles burning throughout the shop, which didn't smell all that bad, in his opinion. Normally, he wasn't too wild about them.

"I think Dinah likes it here because she can let her guard down and be her true self. That's my guess, anyway. Janelle and the other stylists and clients aren't the people Dinah normally hangs around with. I think she feels like she doesn't have to prove anything to them. And I'm hoping that while she's here she opens up to Janelle. I think the cops are probably trying to talk to all of Dinah's regular friends, but I don't know that they'd think to talk to her hairstylist. Or that they'd realize she could turn out to be a true confidante."

"I'm impressed. You may be more of a natural at bounty hunting than either of us realized."

Charlotte gave him a slight smile before turning to a receptionist who was approaching them. Wade took the moment to type a quick text to Maribel asking her to get the word out to everyone that he really needed them to push their informants for reports on Dinah or any of the men he and Charlotte had already encountered while trying to find Dinah.

Wade finished the text as the receptionist was explaining that Janelle was in a storeroom taking inventory. He followed the women through a short hallway to an oversize storage closet. The receptionist left, and after greetings and exchanging a hug, Janelle directed them to her small office, where they could talk.

Charlotte introduced Wade and then wasted no time in explaining why they were there.

"What can you tell us about my sister that might help explain what's happening? Can you maybe give us a direction to start searching for information on people she knew or problems she was dealing with? I know she talked to you about everything. Any small detail could help. *Please*," she added when Janelle was hesitant to respond. "This is a life-or-death situation for Dinah. Her potentially being embarrassed, or getting caught doing something illegal, or being angry with you for betraying a confidence is the least of our worries right now. We *have* to find her and we need all the help we can get."

Janelle took in a deep breath, blew it out and let her shoulders slump. "Okay. There are a couple of things she told me in confidence that concerned me a little bit before, but they really concern me now that she's missing."

"You're doing the right thing," Charlotte assured her.

"She told me about going through some pretty extensive rehab, going to a facility in Colorado, shortly after she left college. I know staying clean and sober was a battle. And I know it was a battle she was losing more often than not, recently. She came in obviously high a few times. I couldn't tell you on what, specifically, each time. But it didn't seem like she enjoyed it. Not really. She seemed sad and disappointed in herself."

There was no missing the fact that Charlotte was fighting back tears. Wade wanted to reach out and wrap an arm around her shoulders and offer her some kind of comfort so badly that the feeling was practically an ache. But he knew better than to give in to the impulse. Especially here and now, when she was working so hard to hold herself together. And when she might still be angry with him, anyway, for his assumption that she didn't understand the way people who weren't rich thought. And he deserved that.

"The other thing I know is that she was worried about money. Which seemed strange at first because, well, you know…" She gave Charlotte an embarrassed smile. "I figured the both of you had rivers of money coming your way all the time. I didn't know until Dinah told me that your parents gave you allowances from the time you were teenagers, but that you had to work at the resort to earn it. That you both had to work for your paychecks now. And that your parents had set up trust funds for you that you can't touch until you turn thirty-five."

Wade almost winced at hearing yet another confirmation that his assumptions about the Halstead twins—

at least in terms of them living a spoiled and completely carefree life—had been wrong.

"So I guess Dinah had whatever income she was paid for managing the coffee shop. I think she said she got a combination of a salary and percentage of the profits. And it wasn't enough to cover what she wanted to buy. Clothes, especially. She liked expensive designer clothes. And jewelry. And luxury travel. You know that.

"She always paid me, which I appreciated. But she complained about money. I joked with her that maybe she shouldn't spend so much, but my comments didn't seem to have any impact. That went on for a while, but then about two months ago, it stopped. She still showed up in a new, very nice outfit whenever she came by to meet me for lunch. But she didn't seem worried. But then, all of a sudden, she was worried about money again."

Janelle shook her head. "That probably sounds scrambled, but I'm just telling you what I noticed, what I saw. I don't know any facts that could explain it."

Wade didn't know the facts, either, but a picture was becoming clearer. Addiction and accompanying bad judgment. Compulsive spending. He didn't want to say anything to Charlotte right now, but maybe it helped to explain how she'd come to be framed for embezzlement. It was possible that Dinah had pilfered money and set her twin up to take the fall. But how did all the assailants figure into this? And what about the resentful cousin and the aggressive investor? Could they have taken advantage of Dinah's issues for their own gain?

Wade felt his phone vibrate. He glanced at the screen while Charlotte and Janelle were saying their goodbyes.

The text he read made his heart speed up. After politely offering his own goodbye to Janelle, he leaned in close to Charlotte as they headed for the door.

"I'm a terrible sister," Charlotte said before he could tell her about the text. "I should have been paying closer attention. Trying harder to understand Dinah."

"We do the best we can," Wade offered. "And when we realize we've fallen short, we try to do better." He took her arm and stopped as they reached the doorway, pausing for a moment to scan their surroundings for signs of danger before they headed outside.

"I've got some news from an informant," he said as soon as they were inside the truck.

"What?" Charlotte asked, her eyes wide and brows lifted in a hopeful expression. "Has someone seen Dinah?"

"No. But we may have a solid lead. My informant works in a bar and grill. He says he's seen Gamble in there a few times with another guy who is presumably a friend. The *friend* was there last night. After eating his dinner and throwing back a couple of drinks, the man ordered some food to take out. Enough for about three or four people. Maybe it's nothing. But it could be something."

"You think Gamble and Murphy are hiding out somewhere with Dinah and this *friend* is bringing them food."

She really was good at thinking like a bounty hunter. "Yes. My informant says he'll call me if the guy shows up again this evening. I think it would be a good idea for both of us to head back to the inn right now. I'll need to organize a crew to be ready to go with us to the bar if I do get the call. We'll follow the guy and see where he goes."

"Please, Lord, let this be the lead that helps us find my sister," Charlotte prayed softly.

"Amen," Wade said in agreement.

He, too, hoped that this would turn out to be the helpful break they were both wishing for.

EIGHT

"Your brother's home really does feel like a refuge," Charlotte said as she and Wade crossed the threshold of the Riverside Inn.

"Yeah, well, for the time being, let's not take safety for granted. Not even here." Wade turned and gave the parking area a quick visual scan before closing the door and engaging the heavy-duty lock. "Paul Boutin won't get paid until you're dead, so he's not going to quit coming after you. Aside from earning his pay, he's got a reputation to defend."

Charlotte drew in a deep breath and tried to settle her nerves. The shooting was the third time she'd been targeted for attack in just as many days. She was fairly certain her sister was in debt to some very dangerous men. And it was possible that Dinah had set things up to make it look like Charlotte had stolen money from the resort.

Happy barks and the sound of dog toenails tapping on the wooden floor greeted them as the resident canines bounded out of the first-floor office and hurried over to offer a boisterous welcome. That helped to lift Charlotte's spirits a little.

After the animals were settled down, she heard Maribel's voice coming from the office. She wore an earpiece and apparently spoke to someone on the phone while pacing in front of an open laptop on Connor's oversize desk. "I just found out that Miller has an ex-wife in that area. I'm texting you her address right now."

"Your mom is on the phone with Connor and Danny." A female voice came from the living room.

A woman with reddish-blond hair—who looked a lot like Danny Ryan—got up from one of the deep cushioned sofas, lifting an elderly-looking black cat from her lap as she stood. "The guys were going to help you out tonight if you got a call from your informant, but then they got a call on their own case and had to take off to hopefully catch their fugitive. So you've got me instead." She offered Charlotte a bright smile. "Jack would have come, too, but he got a call from Milo and Katherine requesting an assist, so of course he had to respond to that. The way things are going, maybe everybody will catch their fugitives today."

"That would be fantastic," Charlotte said.

"I'm Hayley Ryan Colter." She offered Charlotte another smile. "I understand you could use some help right now."

Charlotte nodded. "Yes. Thank you."

Hayley's smile settled into a more serious expression. "I know it can be horrifying to have someone trying to kill you. I *really* know. I've had it happen to me. At times it can look like they have the upper hand, that they have an insurmountable advantage because they skulk in the shadows and repeatedly take you by surprise. But most of them aren't as brilliant as they believe they are. And they can't skulk forever. When the pressure of trying to evade the cops—and us—gets them tired, they start to make mistakes."

"Most of them. You said *most* of them aren't so brilliant."

Hayley shrugged. "Some of them are quite intelligent. It's a shame they turned their talents to crime. But even the smart ones can get overconfident or just plain tired from being on the run. So they stumble. And that's when we pounce on them."

Hayley's words were intense, but also somewhat comforting. It was good to be reminded that the people Charlotte and her family were dealing with were not supervillains with special powers. They were just regular people who were criminals.

"Right now we aren't taking advantage of fugitives stumbling so much as getting hungry," Wade said to his sister. "We're hoping the friend of Gamble's who frequents my informant's bar and grill is bringing him food. And that when we follow the friend, he'll bring us to wherever Gamble and Murphy are hiding Dinah."

The reference to Dinah as a hostage set the pit of Charlotte's stomach squirming again. Fear and anxiety churned and twisted with the other dark emotions and thoughts that she'd tried to keep at bay. Was her assumption that the kidnappers had kept her sister alive based on a false hope?

She was excited by the thought of seeing Dinah again tonight. But that excitement was also tempered by the fear that instead of reuniting with her sister she would instead learn that her twin had perished. That they had been permanently separated before Charlotte ever had the chance to rebuild the strong connection that used to exist between them.

How would she live with that?

"Speaking of people being hungry," Wade said, "let me see if I can find us something to eat around here." He walked toward the kitchen.

Charlotte remained in place and gazed out the window at the deck jutting over the Range River. The sun had dropped low in the west and the view of the shadowy snowcapped mountains in the distance was dramatic and beautiful. Despite the fact that the temperature was dropping fast and it was cold, she would have loved to step outside and have a look around. Maybe shake off those dark thoughts and feelings, at least for a short while. But, as Wade had reminded her, she needed to be careful.

"Don't worry about me," she called out to Wade as he disappeared around a corner. "I don't need anything. I'm not hungry."

"You might want to rethink that." He stepped back around the corner. "If we get a call tonight and have to run, you'll need energy. You can't catch bad guys on just coffee and air."

"He makes a good point," Hayley said quietly to Charlotte. "Not that my *brother* needs to hear any woman telling him he's right." She offered a teasing grin. But then the grin faded. "The call we're waiting for could come in the next few minutes, or it could come sometime after midnight. Maybe we won't get a call at all tonight. But just in case, we've got to be ready to go at the drop of a hat. That means eating enough to keep us going and resting when we can."

Wade strode back out from the kitchen with a package of deli turkey in one hand and a bowl of homemade potato salad in the other. "If we get a call from my informant tonight, you don't have to respond with us. You'd be safer if you stayed. That might be the better choice."

"Nice try at shaking me off, but if the informant calls, I want to go with you. That friend of Gamble's might look familiar to me. Maybe I've seen him around somewhere, and being able to tell the police about that could lead them to further information about what's going on and the rescue of my sister."

Charlotte paused for a moment, deciding that she would focus on helping rescue her twin instead of worrying that the worst possible outcome had already happened. "I changed my mind. I think I would like to have something to eat." She followed Wade into the kitchen.

"Don't forget about me," Hayley called out, trailing behind them. "I'm always ready to eat."

"I know," Wade said without turning around. "That's why I didn't bother to ask."

He collected bread, lettuce and condiments to make the sandwiches while Hayley grabbed plates and cutlery. Not wanting to stand around and be waited on, Charlotte filled glasses with ice and grabbed a pitcher of tea from the refrigerator. She briefly checked in with Maribel, who was busy working on a laptop and said she'd eat later.

It felt good to do something so normal in the midst of everything that had been happening. Just a few short hours ago someone had been shooting at Charlotte and anyone else who got in the way. The hired assassin had escaped only to be able to come after her again.

Charlotte still felt shaky, despite her determination to toughen up so that she could help catch the criminals. When she carried glasses she'd filled with tea to the table, she could see the slight ripples form on the surface as her hands trembled.

Lord, please give me the courage I need.

When she looked up, Hayley caught her eye. The bounty hunter offered a sympathetic smile and then asked, "So, what do you like to do with your time when things are normal?"

When people aren't trying to kill me, you mean. Charlotte chewed her bottom lip for a moment. She appreciated that Hayley was trying to lighten the mood a little, so her first instinct was to make a joke or give some generic answer like hiking in the woods or going boating on the lake.

In the end, she gave in to the unexpected impulse to genuinely share something of herself. She glanced at Wade as he placed the prepared plates on the table and then sat down. After saying grace, they began eating.

"I actually work most of my waking hours these days," Charlotte began. "There was a time when I first moved away for college when I'd decided the family business wasn't for me. But then, things changed. I found a faith I didn't even know I was looking for." She smiled to herself, thinking about how puzzled she'd been at the beginning. How prayer and fellowship had given her insight into so many things that changed her perspective on life, on her family, on how she wanted to live.

"Eventually, I realized I could do a lot of good through working at the Wolf Lake Resort."

"And your parents were agreeable to the idea of focusing on doing good rather than making a profit?" Wade asked, raising an eyebrow. "That's pretty idealistic."

A stab of defensiveness made her regret saying anything. Maybe she should just change the subject. But after a moment, she realized that he wasn't attacking her so much as asking a reasonable question based on what he'd seen of the Halstead family. And what she'd said about them.

"Here's the thing," Charlotte said, setting down her sandwich for a moment. "My degree is in sales and marketing, and while earning it I learned quite a bit about the benefits of doing good when it comes to attracting customers. Supporting literacy programs or animal rescue or neighborhood litter pickups. The sorts of things that everyone can agree are worthwhile.

"When making a decision on where to spend their money, a significant number of people are more strongly drawn to companies that do something like that. So the company benefits, the community benefits and customers feel like they've spent their money wisely. There are also tax benefits for the company. My parents are willing to let me try this out and see where it goes. So I've started with a local literacy program."

Hayley made a sound of agreement. "It's good to have a job where you can be of service somehow."

"Yeah, well, I still have a lot to learn," Charlotte said after eating a bite of her sandwich. "I applied for an internship with a resort down in California, in San Diego, to get some hands-on experience with all of this plus international marketing, as well."

Wade, who'd been eating his potato salad, stopped chewing for a moment. He looked closely at Charlotte, and she braced herself for some sharp comment about her family or the resort or maybe her personally.

"I realize I'm fortunate to be able to go down to San Diego over the summer," she said, figuring that was what he was focusing on. She immediately gave herself a mental kick. She'd been determined not to fall into that old trap of explaining herself so that people would approve of her. Not think that she was spoiled and unappreciative.

"From what I've seen, San Diego is a beautiful city," he said flatly, before taking a sip of his tea. "Maybe you'll find you want to stay."

"Sounds like you're pretty committed to staying here and working with your family," Hayley interjected. She turned to Charlotte. "You're just going for the summer?"

"It's for five months."

Wade nodded without saying anything, his expression shuttering. He continued eating his lunch, but his gaze stayed mostly settled on his food.

Charlotte's heart sank. She'd talked about something important to her and he apparently didn't think much of it. He'd obviously made up his mind about what kind of person she was. He'd probably kept the same opinion that he'd had from the beginning. Which meant those moments when she'd thought they were becoming friends must have only existed in her imagination.

He was helping her because it was his job.

Of course.

Not the first time she'd come up against that hard reality. Probably not the last.

The sinking disappointment in her chest turned edgier, until it felt like shards scratching her heart. So many old thoughts and emotions threatened to overtake and overwhelm her.

No.

She took a deep breath and forced herself to set those feelings all aside. She'd worked too hard to move beyond them. To forge a new path in life where she was strong and pressed into her faith and directed her energy toward a greater good.

What she needed to do right now was focus on keeping herself alive and finding Dinah. She didn't have time for any new *friendships*, anyway. Later, she'd untangle the whole embezzlement accusation fiasco and prove to her family and to the public that she was trustworthy, so that all her plans wouldn't be ruined.

Even though her stomach felt leaden, she made herself continue eating. If all went well, she would be back in the battle to rescue Dinah tonight. After that, she and Wade Fast Horse could go their separate ways.

"Find a table and sit facing toward a wall," Wade said to Charlotte as he held open the door to the bar and grill and she walked past him to go inside. "We don't want this friend of Gamble's to recognize you."

"Understood."

Charlotte had her hair tucked into a beanie and the collar of her jacket flipped up to hide the lower part of her face. The last thing they needed was for the possible kidnappers' accomplice to look around and see someone who was the spitting image of the woman they'd abducted.

Hayley walked in behind Charlotte.

The three settled at a table with a low, flickering candle inside a bottle-shaped holder. A menu was propped up beside it offering a fairly extensive list of appetizers and burgers. Made sense that a lowlife looking for a place to throw down a couple of drinks before grabbing some food to take back to his fellow criminals would repeatedly come here.

Not that they had any proof the man Wade's informant had told them about—he said the guy's name was Larry—was legitimately a person of interest. He could just be a guy who happened to know Gamble and that was all.

Wade glanced toward the bar, where his informant, Shane, was working. The tall, skinny bartender caught Wade's gaze and gave him a slight nod before making a small gesture toward a patron sitting on a stool just a couple of feet away from him.

"Looks like we arrived in time and Larry is still here," Wade said quietly. They'd gotten the call a couple of hours after they'd eaten and hurried over from the inn as quickly as they could.

"I want to get a look at his face and see if I recognize him," Charlotte said.

Wade's gut tightened. It *felt* like a dangerous move, even though his brain told him it probably wasn't. With her pale blond hair covered and in the dim light of the bar, she wouldn't stand out so much. Still, she was a civilian, and if the guy made some kind of aggressive move, she wouldn't know what to do.

Or maybe she would. She'd managed to survive some pretty extreme events over the last couple of days.

Charlotte Halstead was strong, he'd learned. She was tough. She wasn't the pampered and entitled daughter of privilege he'd assumed she was. Charlotte had a lot more character than he'd initially given her credit for. More fight, more compassion, more concern for others.

But she was also going to be leaving town. Never to move back, most likely. San Diego was a big city with a lot going for it. She'd be offered good opportunities while she was working as an intern down there. She'd forget about her plans for her life in Range River, forget about the people in Range River she cared about and who cared for her.

Wade knew exactly how that would go.

Not that he believed *he* was someone in Range River she cared about. Obviously not enough that she would come back for him. He'd thought there might have been a moment here or there when something significant had happened between the two of them, drawing them closer together.

Ridiculous. He shook his head slightly. What had he been thinking?

Besides, people moved on. He *knew* that. For a short while, fascinating Charlotte Halstead had made him want to forget that fact. But he'd come back to his senses.

She would establish her life in a beautiful Southern California beach town. He would remain in Range River.

"I'll go up to the bar with you so you can get a look at this Larry guy," Hayley said to Charlotte. "We'll go to the side where it wraps around so you can try to catch a quick glimpse of him without his noticing. I'll ask the bartender for a couple glasses of water. And then we'll come back to the table. Let's make this quick."

Charlotte nodded. "Okay."

"Try not to stare at him," Wade said as she stood.

"Right."

Wade watched them go. He knew that Hayley was more than capable of looking out for Charlotte should Larry recognize her and try to grab or attack her. But it still didn't make him feel more at ease.

They reached the bar, with Charlotte positioned so

only her profile would be turned toward Larry. She and Hayley got their glasses of water and returned.

"I've never seen him before," Charlotte reported.

So much for the idea that he might have been someone connected to the resort. Abductions by complete strangers were relatively uncommon. That fact continued to stew in the back of Wade's mind.

"I've never seen him before, either," Hayley added. "He's not someone we've dealt with."

"All right. Well, let's follow him when he leaves and see where he goes."

"Should we call Detective Romanov?" Charlotte asked.

"Not yet. It could be this man has no connection to Dinah's disappearance and knows nothing about where Gamble is hiding out right now. Let's see where this takes us."

The fact that Larry had left the bar and grill with a bag of food and then driven to an old motor court on the edge of town had Charlotte's hopes up that they were about to find Dinah. "Seems to me this is the kind of place kidnappers would want to hide somebody."

Charlotte, Hayley and Wade sat in Wade's idling truck, watching as Larry parked at the room farthest from the main office and got out of his car. He walked up to the porch, visible in the light cast by a small fixture, glancing around for a moment before knocking and then being admitted inside.

"Time to let the police know what's going on." Wade grabbed his phone, tapped the screen and put it on speaker setting.

Romanov answered after a couple of rings. "Wade, what have you got for me?"

The bounty hunter explained where they were and what they'd seen.

"Sit tight. I'll be over with a couple of unmarked vehicles. Get the guy's plate number if he leaves. Don't engage with him." She disconnected.

Charlotte gazed out the window, thinking about her sister being held hostage just a few yards away, scared and miserable, having no idea that she was about to be rescued. Charlotte could only guess at the trauma Dinah had suffered through. She couldn't clearly imagine it, but then, she didn't really want to. A wave of guilt washed over her at that realization. At some point if she wanted to help Dinah cope in the aftermath, she would have to make a stronger effort to understand. She might have to sacrifice a bit of her own peace of mind to be of help.

"Breathe," Wade said quietly beside her.

Charlotte filled her lungs, held the air for a few seconds and then blew it out. The action brought her back to the here and now, away from those galloping thoughts of worry and fear for Dinah.

She turned to Wade. There was enough ambient light for her to see his face and those deep brown eyes that were such a fascinating combination of empathetic and assessing. Qualities that worked well together for anyone in his profession, she supposed. Probably beneficial for anyone. They certainly made her feel comforted and protected. At least for the moment.

"It will be all right," Wade said. "Things might happen quickly. If they do, duck down to the floorboard and stay out of sight. Or if you want me to take you away from here right now while things are still quiet, I will."

"I want to be here," Charlotte said. "If my sister is here, I want her to see me. I want her to know that I did everything I could to help find her." Her voice cracked and she blinked back tears. All manner of fear or worry and uncertainty struck her all at once. She was worried for Dinah's safety, for the bounty hunters' safety, and, perhaps selfishly, for her own safety and future. While she absolutely wanted to rescue her sister, and that was 100 percent her goal and priority, finding Dinah would also mean the end of spending time with Wade. And she would miss that. Very much.

She sniffed loudly.

Wade opened the center console and offered up a small box of tissues. She grabbed a few. "Thanks."

"How did you like living on the coast while you were in college?" Hayley asked from the back seat. "I've always thought that would be fun to live near the beach."

Charlotte smiled to herself, appreciating Hayley's effort at using small talk to ease Charlotte's anxiety. She conversed with the bounty hunter about coastal living until a work van pulled up nearby, followed by an older-model SUV.

Wade's phone chimed. "It's Romanov and a couple of plainclothes officers in undercover vehicles," he said after reading the text.

A few more rounds of messages went back and forth. "Okay, two undercover officers are going to knock on the door and pretend they're there to repair something. Romanov wants us to stay back but keep an eye on things in case anyone tries to make a run for it."

"Got it," Hayley answered.

Charlotte's heart raced as two men in jeans and heavy jackets got out of the van. One opened the back door and pulled out a tool kit. At the same time, the SUV that had arrived with them slowly moved forward and then stopped.

Appearing calm and easygoing, the officers chatted as they walked up to the door of the unit Larry had entered earlier, and they knocked.

Charlotte held her breath, waiting to see what happened.

The door opened, light spilled out, and then she saw sudden movement and heard shouting. The doors of the SUV flew open and Detective Romanov and two other cops got out and ran in to assist the undercover officers.

Charlotte's heart leaped into her throat as her whole body tensed, gripped by fear that she would hear gunshots or her sister's screams. But after a few moments, when it got quiet and she couldn't see anything happening, the fear morphed into impatience that practically pushed her out the door.

She reached for the handle, and Wade put his hand on her shoulder. "Wait."

"But I need to see if they found Dinah." Charlotte frantically rushed out the words. "I need to know she's finally okay."

"I know, but we need to hold off for a few minutes, give Romanov and her team time to secure the scene. Approaching officers unexpectedly right after a potentially deadly takedown is not a wise idea."

Charlotte nodded, and then let her chin drop down to her chest. *Dear Lord, please let my sister be okay.*

Wade's phone chimed a couple of minutes later. He looked down and sighed.

"What?" Charlotte demanded, perched on the edge of her seat, ready to leap out and race over to see her sister.

"They've got Gamble and Murphy. And they've arrested Larry for aiding and abetting criminal activity." He looked up. "I'm sorry, but they don't have Dinah. She's not there."

NINE

"We won't stop searching for your sister. The police won't stop, either." Wade had spoken the same sentiment to Charlotte last night while Detective Romanov and her team were wrapping up the scene at the motor court and then again this morning at breakfast. There'd been no sign at all of Dinah, and the criminals had refused to talk. He understood why Charlotte was worried and it made his heart ache to see the sad, hollow expression on her face.

She gave him a distracted nod, as if only vaguely aware that he was in the room and speaking to her.

The two of them were seated on a sofa in the den that served as Connor's office at the Riverside Inn. Connor was there, as were Hayley and Danny. Connor stood by his desk, leaning against it, while Maribel sat in the desk chair with an electronic tablet, poised to take notes.

Breakfast had been quiet, with Charlotte moving her food around on her plate rather than eating it. Wade didn't blame her. Many times over the last two days he'd found himself imagining how he'd feel if one of his adoptive siblings were missing. Devastated, obviously. Just thinking about the very remote possibility tensed the pit of his stomach.

For Charlotte to have her hopes built up last night only to have them resoundingly dashed must have been gutting. He shook his head and took a deep breath. Caring about someone—Charlotte, in this case—and having to watch them suffer repeatedly while being unable to ease their pain or do anything to help them was a horrible feeling.

Wade had gone through a similar situation as a kid, watching his mom get hurt over and over again as his dad made promises of his imminent return from faraway California that never came through. Somewhere along the line Wade had made the decision to give up hope. Or at least give up hope when it came to his own personal relationships. The kind of relationships where you more or less handed your life to another person and trusted that they would take care of it.

Looking at Charlotte right now, recognizing the expression of someone on the verge of hopelessness, it struck him how utterly pointless that was. To give up hope in situations where possibilities for a good outcome still existed, even if they appeared only slightly probable at the moment.

Of course he had hope in terms of his faith, in terms of redemption and a better life to come. But did having that kind of hope get him off the hook for daring to have more hope in this lifetime? Right now, finding himself unexpectedly revisiting thoughts and feelings he hadn't considered in a while, he wasn't so sure.

This was certainly an awkward moment to realize that despite his concerns about Charlotte's social station in life, and his own, and about her plans to leave Range River for an internship down in California, he still dared to care about her. Enough to risk hoping that once this case was resolved, she might find that she cared about him, too.

"Still no word from Detective Romanov?" Charlotte asked him.

Wade shook his head.

"Romanov is a good interviewer." Danny sat in an upholstered chair beside Connor's desk. "She's highly motivated to solve cases and obtain convictions. It's early in the process. She'll get information out of Gamble and Murphy. Maybe their buddy Larry. Offer plea deals if she has to."

"What if Dinah wasn't there because they killed her and buried her somewhere?" Charlotte's voice sounded strangely monotone.

It was something Wade had already considered. He was fairly sure the rest of the bounty hunters had considered it, as well.

"That is a possibility," Connor acknowledged.

Wade cut him a dark glance. It was so like Connor not to sugarcoat things.

"But that doesn't strike me as likely," Connor continued. "What would be the point? There's obviously a conspiracy going on here—between Gamble and Murphy, plus a professional hit man, and possibly including several other people—and this clearly isn't some personal crime of passion sort of situation. Beyond that, to a criminal's way of thinking, your sister would be a person of value because she comes from a family with money. They'd need to keep her alive to get paid."

"But there's been no ransom demand," Hayley interjected.

Connor nodded at his sister. "Not that we know of. Maybe a demand was sent to her parents and they've kept it under wraps." He settled his gaze on Charlotte. "Or they could have sent a demand to her boyfriend. Any of them could be manipulated by threats to keep things secret."

"We have solid reasons to keep pushing forward," Hayley said to Charlotte.

"But we need to update our strategy." Wade had been pondering how to resume the chase and discover new leads. "Do deeper online dives into Gamble's and Murphy's backgrounds. Especially their criminal associates. Maybe we'll find someone with a history of extortion. We should increase the amount of cash we're offering our informants. See if that motivates them to look a little harder for information to give us. And, of course, we need to put energy in finding the hit man who came after us at the coffee shop. Paul Boutin. He's a legitimate target for us since he's a bail jumper. Beyond that, if we find out who hired him, that might lead us to whoever has taken Dinah."

"Looking into the embezzlement fiasco could help." Charlotte held up her phone. "There's a new *anonymously sourced* rumor in the online newspaper. I suppose acknowledging it as just a rumor protects them legally. But the damage is done to my reputation, nevertheless."

"Jonah wasn't able to learn anything about the source of the original embezzlement rumors through his connections at the online newspaper, so I'll visit their offices and see if I can learn anything," Maribel said. "The arrest of Gamble and Murphy is a big, legitimate news story. If I offer them some previously unknown detail about how that went down in return for information on how they received the embezzlement rumors, maybe they'll go for it. With everything else that's been happening to Charlotte and Dinah, you'd think they'd take their reporting of all of this more seriously."

Charlotte made a scoffing sound. "They're just interested in sensational headlines that get clicks and make them money."

"It's easy enough to be flippant at a keyboard or over the phone," Maribel continued. "But having someone show up in person to talk to the managing editor might make them take things more seriously. Or I could mention that I'm willing to pay for information loudly enough that anyone in the office can hear. Somebody might contact me after that."

"I appreciate everything all of you are doing to help," Charlotte said, glancing around the room. "While you're trying to track down leads and information, I'm going to be at the resort talking with my parents."

Charlotte's words set off an internal alarm for Wade. Gamble and Murphy had been captured, but Boutin was still at large. Perhaps their arrest had led to the cancellation of the assassination order. But maybe not. It wasn't a chance worth taking. "Can't you just talk to your parents on the phone?" He really wanted Charlotte to remain safely hidden at the inn.

She held up her phone, a pinched expression on her face. "My dad messaged me about the news article regarding Gamble's and Murphy's arrests. I told him the police didn't get any new information about Dinah's whereabouts. He said that he and Mom want to see for themselves that I'm safe." She shrugged. "I'd say he wants to make sure I'm safe *and* he wants to talk about his missing money." She offered a sad smile. "I'm not sure which is the higher priority."

Wade's face heated as he thought about how Charlotte's parents seemed to undermine her sense of value. Maybe Dinah felt the same weak sense of support, and that was what drove her addiction issues. He obviously had no way of knowing anything about that. But he did know that there were people in town—or maybe from out of town—who wanted the Halstead money and resort property. And anyone attempting to get to that wealth through the Halstead twins would remain a serious threat to Charlotte.

"The money was transferred into your personal account and yet you've said nothing about it." Arthur Halstead let his words hang in the air. It wasn't exactly a direct accusation, but it felt like one. He stood in front of a window in his office, backlit by the bright sunlight outside so that it was hard for Charlotte to see his face.

Charlotte's parents had hugged her when she and Wade first arrived at the reception area outside their office suite. They'd asked her if she was okay, told her she looked like she'd lost weight and expressed concern over the bruises still visible on her face. Ethan had been there as well, looking even worse than Charlotte felt, practically begging for updates on the hunt for Dinah. When Charlotte had to tell him she didn't really have news about her sister at all, he'd looked crushed.

Inside Arthur's office, with the door shut and only Wade to witness the conversation between Charlotte and her parents, the communications from Arthur and Kandace to their daughter became cooler. Kandace had directed Wade to wait outside the office while they talked, but Charlotte had insisted he come along with her. She felt stronger with Wade by her side. Beyond that, he was sharp and attentive and might notice some detail she missed.

Charlotte shook her head in response to her father's insinuating comment. "I didn't realize the money was in my account."

"Don't you get notifications on your phone?"

"I have all kinds of messages on my phone that I haven't paid attention to because I've been busy and tired and had other things on my mind."

"And yet you saw your father's message about the news story this morning," Kandace said.

"Yeah, because we're *family* and that's supposed to mean something. And maybe that could be expressed by something like, oh, I don't know, prioritizing a response to messages from each other because it might be important."

Kandace tapped her lacquered fingernails on the armrest of her chair. "You don't need to get snippy, Charlotte. We're all under stress and worried about Dinah. And before you try to imply otherwise, no, the money is not more important than finding your sister. But it's the only situation we can do anything about."

Kandace's voice broke on the last few words and tears began to slide down her face.

Guilt hung around Charlotte's shoulders like an old weighted blanket. Her parents weren't completely unfeeling monsters, but they were so wrapped up in their business at times that they lost some of their capacity for a deeper connection and empathy when it came to their children. So much of their time was tied up in numbers and reports and scheduling and not wasting time on *silly* things. Never mind that those silly things—like hopes and dreams and a kid's desire to figure out who she was—were important to other people. To children. To the Halstead twins as they were growing up.

She glanced over at Wade, expecting to see judgment. He probably thought she was a jerk. The disconnect she oftentimes felt with her parents was such a subtle thing and they put on such a good front that no one else ever saw it. A circumstance that often made Charlotte feel very alone.

To her surprise, she saw acceptance in Wade's eyes. He gave her a slight nod of encouragement. He *understood*.

Charlotte took a deep breath, reminding herself that her parents were as bewildered as she was by the events of the past few days. Even if they hadn't been forced to withstand the literal physical attacks that she'd faced. "If I had used my laptop to go into Accounting and used the payroll program to put money into my own account, don't you think I would have immediately moved it somewhere else to hide it? I haven't had anything to do with this, so it's probably still sitting there."

She took out her phone, tapped the screen a few times and pulled up her personal bank account. The balance remained way beyond normal. She showed the screen to her parents. "I don't have the necessary access to move it back into the corporate payroll account, but you can do that or have someone in Accounting do it." She looked up at them. "Am I right in assuming you're still looking into how this happened? You didn't simply assume I'd stolen it?"

Her father pursed his lips. "Well, we wanted to explore all possibilities before going further with the forensic audit."

"Just in case I'd had something to do with it?"

After a pause, her father nodded.

She was trying hard to be gracious, and finally decided that, in their own way, her parents were actually trying to be loving and protect her by potentially covering for her. And she supposed it was maybe sweet, in an odd kind of way. And that maybe, under their hard exterior, they had a tenderness she hadn't appreciated. Like anyone else, they could only be how they were.

"Mrs. Halstead, has anyone contacted you with a ransom demand?"

For a moment Kandace looked as if she'd forgotten Wade was in the room. "No," she finally said, wiping her eyes and recovering her controlled, professional expression. "If they had, we would have paid it." She exchanged looks with her husband. "We've expected that from the time Dinah went missing and we've made preparations to get cash quickly if we need to."

An awkward few moments of silence followed. There really wasn't much Charlotte's parents could do other than wait and do their best to be ready for anything. Charlotte, on the other hand, could keep working with Wade as they did their best to track down her sister.

"We should go." Charlotte got to her feet and Wade stood alongside her.

She gave both of her parents lingering hugs goodbye. And each of them seemed to melt their former defense stance while in her embrace.

A few minutes later Charlotte and Wade stepped out of the resort and walked to his truck. As usual, his head was on a swivel as he continually kept track of their surroundings. Having learned her lesson, Charlotte likewise remained vigilant. There was a payoff for being paranoid these days, she reminded herself, as she shifted her gaze and noticed the plants and trees beginning to put forth blooms and leaves. The weather had warmed up considerably over the last two days, and the bright sunshine was a welcome contrast to the dark gloom that felt like it had dropped over Range River since the night Murphy had kidnapped her.

"I'm going to take you back to the inn and then I'm going to go talk to a few informants," Wade said as they turned from the parking lot and drove down the road that would take them through town and beyond, to the open and undeveloped stretches of land near the inn.

"You don't believe I would be of any help," Charlotte said flatly.

"No, I don't. Not with what I have planned for the rest of the day. The people I intend to visit will be *less* likely to talk in front of you. Or anyone else, for that matter. Their anonymity is important to them and I respect that."

"I understand," Charlotte said. There were things that were more important than Charlotte feeling like she was helping. This was probably a time where the most helpful thing she could do would be to stay out of the way.

He glanced over, like he needed to confirm that she meant it. So she summoned up a slight smile and nodded.

"I'm going to see if I can find out if Gamble and Murphy have any known enemies. If so, I'll try to track down those enemies and see what I can learn. Those are the kinds of people who would happily tell me everything I want to know. I'll do the same thing regarding Paul Boutin."

"That will be a lot of interviewing. I'm not complaining, but that will take a lot of time."

"I might be able to get Hayley's husband, Jack, at Eagle Rapids Bail Bonds, to help out."

Charlotte tried to push back against the sensation of chilly fear that was settling over her. Dinah had been missing for over forty-eight hours now and Charlotte had watched enough true crime stories on TV to know that was very, very bad. She could only hope that Detective Romanov and her team had some helpful information they hadn't shared with her and the bounty hunters.

Bam!

Charlotte heard a rifle shot. The truck shook and the front passenger side dropped down. The vehicle swerved to the side as Wade fought with the steering wheel to gain control.

"Get down!"

Charlotte scrambled down to the floorboard.

Bam! A second shot blew out the front tire on the driver's side, forcing Wade to stop.

Bam! Bam! Bam!

The added shots struck metal on the passenger side of the truck around the front and fender, making menacing thunking sounds as they moved toward the door beside Charlotte.

Sheer terror sent her shrinking down as far as she could go, curling up into a tight ball. Her heart nearly pounded out of her chest as she fervently prayed. *Please, Lord, help!*

The front windshield was struck twice, the bullets bursting through at the impact points while the surrounding safety glass shattered with a few splintery pieces breaking away.

"The truck's undrivable and we can't stay here." Wade was stretched across the bench seat, trying to stay out of view, his head toward Charlotte. "We have to get out. It looks like the shooter is on your side. I need you to get up and move in my direction."

Charlotte stared at him. Fear had locked most of her muscles tight. She'd barely been able to turn her head to look in his direction when he spoke to her. How could she possibly get up and out of the truck? Much less be able to run for cover?

"We can do this," Wade said, seeming to read her thoughts. His tone was urgent, but calm. He held his hands toward her. "We need to move while there's a lull in the shooting."

Charlotte imagined the assassin reloading. Or creeping closer to the truck until he felt the time was right to boldly step up and aim directly at her through the window before he finished her off.

A shudder passed through her body.

There seemed to be no safe option. She couldn't think of a way out of the situation that didn't involve taking a potentially fatal risk.

She looked at Wade's outstretched hands. Thought about her prayer, which she'd already silently repeated several times. Maybe this was a situation where she'd have to rely on another person to get the help she'd prayed for. Much as she disliked doing that, much as she wanted to resolve situations herself, much as she feared depending on someone and being bitterly disappointed, yet again, that was something she had to do. *Now.*

She reached for Wade's hands, let him help pull her up until he had to let go to open the door and back out. It was only for a few seconds, but his touch was enough to revive her, to break the hold of fear and get her moving and thinking again.

Wade hunkered down, using his open door as a shield. Charlotte climbed out until she was beside him.

Bam! The shot blasted through the passenger side window.

Wade grabbed her hand and they ran across the other lane in the street, heading for a cluster of trees with a dense thicket woven through them.

Charlotte heard a low rumble of traffic as cars approached from the direction of town. She moved slightly to look around the tree trunk she was hiding behind and saw the shadowy form of a man wearing a knit cap and dark glasses near the truck. He turned his head back and forth until he caught sight of her.

Paul Boutin. The hit man.

He holstered his pistol and reached around for the rifle that hung on a strap over his shoulder. When he lifted it and took a shooter's stance, Charlotte quickly ducked back behind the tree.

Seconds later, she heard the crack of a shot. At almost the same time, she heard a car whizzing by and the clank of a round striking metal. Charlotte took another look as the car veered off the side of the road, crashing into a tree. Her heart dropped at the realization the driver must be hurt.

A second driver rounded the curve, slowed and pulled to the side of the road by the crash site. That driver probably had no idea what had just happened and wasn't aware of the danger of being shot.

Meanwhile, the hit man had disappeared.

"Stay here in case Boutin is still lurking around and call 9-1-1," Wade said. "I'm going to go help the driver of that crashed car."

The occupants of the second car were already out of

their vehicle and checking on the injured driver. Wade hurried over to assist. Together, the responders managed to force the driver's crumpled door open. It looked as if he was bleeding and trying to get out of the car. Wade and the others encouraged him to stay put until an ambulance arrived.

By that time Charlotte had already punched in the emergency number and given the operator the specifics of what had happened. Emergency medical services appeared quickly, along with two police patrol cars. At that point, Charlotte reasoned it was safe for her to come out from hiding.

The driver of the wrecked car was not seriously injured by the gunshot or the crash, it turned out. The sound of the bullet striking his vehicle had startled him so badly that he'd swerved and struck the tree and been slightly cut by broken glass.

Meanwhile, officers had begun a search of the area for the gunman. Based on past experience and the fact that he was a professional, Charlotte had no doubt Paul Boutin had put an exit strategy in place ahead of time and was now long gone.

"Do you think Boutin saw us go to the resort and assumed we would come back along this route?" Charlotte asked Wade as they waited for a tow truck. "Could that be how he knew exactly where and when to find us?"

"Maybe. It's also possible that someone at the resort told him we were there. Knowing that gave him the information he needed to set up the ambush."

Charlotte sighed heavily. She didn't want to believe that someone at the resort had set her up for assassination. Didn't want to accept the possibility that someone she knew and trusted was behind every terrible thing that had been happening. Including the disappearance of her twin.

She'd tried to laugh off Wade's previous suggestions that someone close to her and her family was the one wreaking havoc on their lives. Now it looked like she had to seriously consider that possibility if she wanted to keep herself and her sister alive.

TEN

After having his truck towed from the shooting scene, Wade called Maribel to give him and Charlotte a ride back to the inn. Then he borrowed a company vehicle and set out to locate the potential useful informants he'd mentioned to Charlotte.

When he arrived back at the Riverside Inn after being away most of the afternoon, the first thing he did once he walked through the front door was to go looking for Charlotte. He realized it was highly unlikely that she would have been in danger while he was gone, and if something untoward had happened, he would have been notified. Nevertheless, he wanted to see her.

Maybe it wasn't so much that he'd been worried, but rather that he'd felt something missing as he'd worked in town without her. And that was an odd experience for him. He had friends, he certainly wasn't antisocial, but letting a woman get close enough that he didn't feel quite 100 percent without her was not normal for him.

Nothing about this situation, or relationship, or whatever it was, was normal for him.

For one thing, while she wasn't exactly a client, this thing between them that had them spending so much time together *was* a business arrangement of sorts. And Wade did not mix business with his social life. And for another, despite how down-to-earth she seemed, she *was* one of the Halsteads. A fact he was reminded of several times today as he drove around to talk to various informants and constantly saw the resort tower on the edge of Wolf Lake.

He walked into the kitchen thinking Charlotte might be in there. Instead, he only saw Maribel, who was starting dinner. "Hi, Mom."

She turned to smile at him. "Did you drum up any good leads?"

He offered a half shrug in response. "You know how it is. People give you pieces of information. You can't see the big picture, so you don't know how to put it all together. Not until you learn that one specific detail that ties everything together."

"Well, keep pushing until you learn that detail." She picked up an onion and began peeling it.

"I handed out a fair amount of cash with the promise of more in return for some solid information. We'll see how that goes." He grabbed a bottle out of the refrigerator. "It seems odd to me that no one's been able to tell me anything so far. Lowlifes like to brag about their accomplishments as much as anybody else. Seems odd that nobody's overheard anything." He took a swig of water. "Or maybe they're just afraid to talk about it."

"It might be a very small number of people are involved and they're being smart about it," Maribel suggested as she started chopping the onion. "Or one of your earlier suspicions could be true. Maybe the Invaders motorcycle gang is involved. They're pretty tight-lipped."

"Could be an even tighter clique than that," Wade said grimly.

"What do you mean?"

"My gut instinct is telling me that a family member, a business associate or someone she believes is a friend is involved. Possibly involved in planning the whole thing. I've tried to talk to Charlotte about it a little. She wanted to dismiss the idea out of hand at first. But now she's starting to consider it." He took another drink of water. "I feel mean encouraging her to think about who might have betrayed her and her family. I know it's painful for her. But I also think it's possible if she considers the idea long enough she'll be able to point out someone we should spend more time investigating."

Betrayal by someone you knew and loved was the worst. Wade knew that from experience.

"Sounds like you're already on the follow-the-money trail." Maribel slid the chopped onion from the cutting board into a pan of warm oil and it started to sizzle. "Putting together a timeline is always a good idea, too. Sometimes it directs your attention toward something you hadn't thought of before."

While Maribel had never been an actual bounty hunter herself, she had spent plenty of time conducting interviews, doing online research and brainstorming with the bounty hunters. Over time, she'd developed a pretty sharp insight into how to find people.

Wade reached for a corn-bread muffin cooling on the countertop. "I need to talk to the others. Touch base and see what they've learned from their informants."

"Connor should be home in about an hour or so. Danny and Hayley will be here for dinner tonight, too."

Wade nodded. "Good. Where's Charlotte?" He'd

waited a while to ask, because he didn't want his growing interest in her to be obvious.

Of course, he didn't fool his mom, and the hint of a smile playing across Maribel's lips told him so. "Last I saw her, she was on the deck taking in some sun now that it's finally warmed up a bit."

Wade quickly finished drinking his bottle of water and then headed across the great room to open the slider to the deck.

Charlotte glanced over. "Hi."

For some dumb reason, he experienced a flutter of emotion that felt like, but couldn't possibly be, nervousness. "Hello."

"I came out to get a little bit of sun and try to cheer myself up."

"Is it helping?"

"Not much."

Tall, potted evergreen shrubs kept on the deck for purposes of providing security had been arranged to form a screen directly in front of Charlotte so that no one could see her and take a shot at her from the other side of the river.

Seeing that she was safely situated, he dropped into the chair beside her.

She had a novel in her lap, but before Wade opened the door he'd seen that she wasn't reading it. She'd been looking toward the end of the deck, where there was no evergreen barrier and the wide river was visible. The ground was fairly rocky in places, and depending on the weather and season, the waters could be flowing at a steady and smooth rate or they could be splashing in a swiftly raucous and unpredictable pattern. Either way, the view of the mountains in the distance was always calming. At least, that was his experience.

"I don't suppose you found Dinah while you were out today," Charlotte said dully.

"I'm sorry, but no, I didn't."

She turned to him, her face pale and her features appearing nearly statue-like in their stony fear. "Don't apologize. That came out sounding like I might be disappointed in you when I'm really disappointed in myself. I can't help thinking that all of this involves my family and that means I should have somehow seen it coming. I should have known Dinah was in some kind of trouble."

"We're going to have to agree to disagree on that one. Sometimes family members are the hardest people to understand. Even if you see them fairly often, you don't always pick up on the changes in them. Or maybe you just don't want to see them."

Her loyalty impressed him. Even under the immense stress of having repeatedly been attacked and having her sister missing, even with her parents believing she could have embezzled money from the family business, she still cared about them. Still wanted to protect them and still felt responsible to look after them to some degree. Loyalty was a trait Wade very much admired. Something that seemed to be in short supply in the world, at times.

"Were any of your informants able to tell you anything useful?"

"A few random bits of information. Where Gamble likes to hang out when he's not locked up. The part of town where Boutin has been seen fairly often recently."

"Well, that's something."

"After Connor gets home and Danny and Hayley

show up for dinner, we'll compare notes and see if we get an idea of where to look next for Dinah and Boutin. Finding either one could help lead us to the other. But know that I realize finding Dinah is the priority."

"I'd hoped Detective Romanov would call and tell me Gamble and Murphy finally started talking and gave her some information about my sister, but I never heard from the detective."

"I went by the police department and spoke with her. Gamble started to answer some of her questions, and in return the city prosecutor is putting together a plea deal so he'll be motivated to talk more. The stuff Gamble has been saying hasn't been investigated or confirmed, so it's not to be completely believed yet."

"What's he saying?"

"He's claiming that your sister really does owe him a significant amount of money. Apparently he's been expanding his burglary career into a loan-sharking enterprise. When he loaned Dinah the money and she stopped making any effort to pay him back, he figured he had to do something splashy. He wanted to scare her into paying him *and* he wanted to send a message. He wanted his other clients to see that it was dangerous not to pay him, plus he wanted the other goons in town to see that he wasn't a pushover. Otherwise, the criminals would come after him and his business."

"That all makes sense, but it doesn't explain why he came after me."

"He still claims that he and Murphy thought you were Dinah, originally. After that first kidnapping attempt fell apart, they figured Dinah would be extra vigilant and possibly surrounded by resort security staff because she knew he was after her. They decided to go after you because they thought you'd be easier to get to. The plan was to grab you and demand the money they were owed as a ransom. They figured Dinah would find a way to pay up. Get the money from your parents, if she had to."

"But what about Dinah's disappearance? Or the hit man trying to kill me? Or the embezzlement?"

Wade shook his head. "I don't know. Gamble isn't saying anything more until he gets his plea deal."

Charlotte tapped her fingers on the arms of her chair. "The men who started everything are locked up, and yet I'm still the target for assassination." She shook her head. "Someone hired a professional killer to come after me and Dinah's still missing." Her voice began to shake. "Instead of making progress, it feels like we're going backward. That things are getting *worse*."

"We'll find Dinah, we'll find Paul Boutin and we'll find whoever hired Boutin," Wade said, wanting to reassure himself as much as he wanted to reassure Charlotte. "The cops are on this. We're on this. At any moment we could get a break and wrap up this case."

The look in Charlotte's tear-filled eyes said it all. She wasn't buying his comforting words. And honestly, he was having a little trouble believing them himself.

Charlotte was sitting at the dinner table, moving her food around on her plate without eating much, when she heard her phone chime in her pocket, indicating an incoming call. Normally, she would ignore her phone at the dinner table. But with Dinah missing, she was desperate for any helpful information.

She froze in indecision, not wanting to be disrespectful to the people who had welcomed her into their home.

The main members of the Range River Bail Bonds team were seated at the table around her. Beside her, Wade offered an encouraging nod. "Go ahead and answer it if you want to."

Charlotte grabbed the phone and glanced at the screen. "It's from an unknown number." She looked up and locked gazes with Wade. It could turn out to be something inconsequential, like a wrong number or an automated sales call. Nevertheless, hope and fear warred within her. Could this be the good news she'd hoped for telling her that Dinah was okay? Or would it be yet another player in whatever weird game was going on, calling to make a ransom demand?

"Excuse me." Charlotte got up and stepped toward the living room to take the call. Behind her, she heard the scrape of Wade's chair as he got up to follow her.

Charlotte tapped the screen. "Hello?"

"You answered! I thought I was going to have to leave a message."

The connection wasn't great, but Charlotte still recognized the voice. *"Dinah?"*

"Put it on speaker," Wade said, standing beside her.

The rest of the crew quietly moved toward them from the dining room.

"Is it really you?" Charlotte said after tapping the screen. Her heart thundered in her chest and her pulse pounded in her ears as she waited for what felt like a very long time before hearing a reply.

"Hey, sis, how are you?"

It *was* Dinah. And she sounded so normal.

It was the last thing Charlotte expected. She shook her head to clear her confusion. "How am I? How are

you? *Where* are you? What happened? Are you okay?"
The questions poured out of her.

"I'm fine." There was a slight delay before she added,
"I just needed to get away for a few days and clear my
head."

What?

"Clear your head? Are you saying you just left? Of
your own free will?" Anger and stunned disbelief bat-
tled in Charlotte's mind as she tried to understand what
her sister was saying.

"Yeah. A couple of hours after you went to bed, I
called Lyndsay Mercer. I wanted to slip away for a while.
I didn't want to get into a big debate about it with Mom
and Dad or Ethan or you. I just wanted to go. So I dressed
in drab clothes and a hat so I wouldn't stand out in the
dark. I left through the back door and kept my gaze
turned downward so my face wouldn't show up on any
security cameras. I didn't have to go far to reach the forested area of the property where I'd be hidden by trees,
and then I crossed the half mile or so to the city road
where Lyndsay was waiting for me. She picked me up
and gave me a ride to the east end of the lake. Her parents have a pretty little summerhouse out there where
it's quiet and I—"

"We thought you had been kidnapped!" Frustration
flashed hot through Charlotte like a wildfire. So many
times her sister had been selfish and self-absorbed. And
here she was, doing it again at a great cost, emotionally,
and in terms of the dollar expense for the police and
others to search for her. "You left everything behind.
It looked like you'd left against your will."

"Oh sorry." Dinah cleared her throat. "I was kind
of high when I realized I'd been playing around with

drinking and a few other things way too much. I blamed myself for you getting kidnapped and decided I needed to get myself together. I wanted to go someplace quiet to do it."

You're right to blame yourself for the kidnapping. It happened because of the foolish decisions you made.

"I wanted to get away from the resort and everybody and everything going on there," Dinah continued. "Someplace kind of isolated seemed best and I knew Lyndsay's family had just inherited the house from her grandpa. I knew if I took my phone and credit cards I'd just give in to temptation again once my high wore off." There was a long pause and then she added, "I didn't want to say anything to Mom and Dad. Or Ethan. I couldn't stand to see the looks of disappointment on their faces."

Please, Lord, give me patience and understanding. Charlotte took a deep breath and looked up at the ceiling for a moment. Her cheeks were warm and she knew she was about to lose her temper.

"How is it that she's able to call now?" Wade asked quietly.

"Is someone there with you?" Dinah had apparently heard him.

Charlotte was about to unload all the details about the bounty hunters and the police and the attempts on her life and everything, when she caught Wade shaking his head. He held up a scrap of paper where he'd written, "Tell her I'm just a friend."

Just a friend. The truth was he was so much more. But Wade and all the other bounty hunters wore strangely reserved expressions. That didn't look happy or relieved that Dinah was okay. Obviously Charlotte felt a more tumultuous mix of emotions, but that was because her sister had behaved like a thoughtless jerk and Charlotte had a right to take more personal offense. She would have expected the bounty hunters to be glad this particular job was over.

"That's just a friend I met through the literacy project," Charlotte fibbed. By now Wade had scratched out a note saying "Ask her how she is able to call now," so she voiced his question.

"The second day I was here I discovered a prepay phone her family leaves up here just in case they need it. Turns out you have to stand in exactly the right spot to get connectivity."

"And you're just calling *now*?"

"Well, yeah," Dinah responded in a snippy tone. "The point was to *not* call anyone. To just dry out a little on my own. And I did."

"And now?"

"Now I need you to come get me."

"I'll do that. But first I need to call the police and let them know you're okay. And Mom and Dad. And Ethan. I need to tell them, too."

"No! Wait, please. I want you to come get me."

Wade reached for Charlotte's arm, and then leaned in to whisper directly into her ear. "We need to call the police. This could be some kind of trap."

Charlotte turned to stare at him. He thought Dinah would set her up to be hurt or killed? "My sister can be an idiot," Charlotte whispered into Wade's ear. "But she's not vicious."

"She could be doing this against her will. The hit man—or somebody—could have a gun pointed at her head."

He was right. The hired assassin had tried to kill Charlotte just a few hours ago. And, as a less substantial point but still one to be considered, there was the embezzlement situation. There was some kind of larger plot going on. Her main focus had been on finding her twin sister, but Dinah being missing was not the only danger at hand. There was something else going on, too. But it was all too shadowy for her to see it.

"Charlotte?" Dinah's voice carried through the phone. She sounded worried, Charlotte thought. Scared.

"I'm here."

"Please don't call the police yet. Or Mom and Dad. Because they will call the police and I don't want that. Not just yet."

"Why?"

Dinah sighed. "Look, now that my mind has cleared, I realize what I did was stupid. But honestly, at the time, I thought it was the best thing. And I wanted to act fast, before I lost the will to do it." She sighed again, heavily. "I really, really want to get myself together. I'm sorry that what I did put you in danger. That will never, *ever* happen again."

Was that true? Would her sister never put her in danger? Or was she in danger herself? Could it be that she was lying and she was under the influence right now?

"If you call the police, they'll send a car out here. Some wannabe photojournalist with a blog or their own gossip site or whatever will follow them. They'll end up getting pictures of me and posting them and I'll be humiliated and I just can't stand that." Dinah started to cry. "I really am doing my best here. And I'll answer for everything. Just…please help me with this."

"Okay. Where are you?"

From the corner of her eye, Charlotte could see Wade's expression darken with suspicion.

Dinah gave her an address. "You'll like it out here," she added hopefully, as if trying to lighten the mood of the conversation a little. "It's got a hippie vibe. There's a cute little gazebo in the front yard. Since the weather's nice, I'll wait for you out there. I'll be all packed up and I can just jump into your SUV and we can go."

"See you in a bit." Charlotte disconnected.

"This is not a good idea," Wade said gravely. "It has all the markings of an ambush."

Charlotte nodded. "I understand. And if you don't want to go with me, I understand that, too. But I'd really like all of you to help me with this." She took in everyone with a sweeping glance. "You know what? It's easy to be loving and forgiving to someone who looks like a victim. It's harder to be that way with someone who's made a mistake. A big one." She took a deep breath. "I'm angry with Dinah right now." She shook her head. "You can't imagine how angry."

She crossed her arms over her chest and hugged herself. "We can call the cops shortly after we get there, if you want. Bring Dinah to the police station if Detective Romanov asks us to. But first, I want to give Dinah a little bit of a chance. Let her hold on to a little bit of her dignity, if that is what this request is really about. Or let her confess to me first if she's done something illegal. Give her a chance to get it off her chest and explain before we go to the police. Because I don't intend to help her hide any wrongdoing."

They didn't need to hear her fairly lengthy, sad story about being alienated from her identical twin sister for so long. Or about how much she wanted to reforge that connection. If that reconnection had to happen in a situation like this, where Charlotte took the first step, maybe even the biggest step, or the most steps toward reconciliation, so be it. She'd prayed for the opportunity to repair her relationship with Dinah. Maybe this awkward, murky situation was part of the answer to that prayer.

Wade, Maribel, Danny, Connor and Hayley all exchanged glances with one another while Charlotte stood there waiting for their decision.

One by one, they each gave a slight nod.

"Looks like we're all going with you," Wade said. "But you have to agree not to take any chances with your own safety."

Charlotte offered what felt like a bleak smile. "I'll do my best."

ELEVEN

"Looks like we're almost there." Charlotte turned her gaze from the GPS screen on the dash to glance at their surroundings. Wade was driving an SUV that belonged to Range River Bail Bonds while his truck was being repaired.

Darkness had fallen over the forested area at the eastern end of Wolf Lake. The terrain was much rockier than it was in town, and the narrow highway they were driving alternately dipped and rose, as well as curving back and forth, as it followed the edge of the lake.

"Don't get out of the vehicle the moment we arrive," Wade said, his voice tight with tension. "Even if you see Dinah, and she's alone, and everything looks fine. Wait. Give us a moment to make certain the location is secure and that this meeting isn't some kind of trap she's being forced to set against her will." He turned to her. *"Please."*

"Of course."

She meant to keep her word, though it would be a challenge. She wanted so much to hug her sister and know that she was okay. At the same time, she wanted to demand answers for the questions still swirling around in her mind. She was determined not to lose her temper, but she also wanted to make certain her twin truly understood the gravity of what she'd done. How many people she'd upset, how much time had been wasted by authorities as they'd searched for her. So many things needed to change in Dinah's behavior. For that matter, the whole way her family interacted needed to be adjusted in the wake of this string of horrible events. Charlotte offered a brief prayer for that to happen. Immediately, if possible.

The GPS indicated that they'd arrived at their final turn. It led them onto a private unpaved road with a wide curve shortly after turning off the highway. From there it continued downhill, around a couple of large rock outcroppings, toward the shore of the lake.

Lights flickered through the SUV's interior as the pickup truck following them passed over a bump in the road. Connor, Danny and Hayley Ryan were in there.

"I'm going to let Dinah know that we're here. Now that she knows about the attacks that have been launched on me, she might be scared when she sees unfamiliar vehicles driving up." She reached for her phone and tapped the screen to call the number Dinah had used earlier.

A recording told her the call didn't go through. She tried again, with the same result. "Well, she did say she had connectivity issues out here," Charlotte said, feeling uneasy even though there were plenty of locations around the lake where reception was spotty.

"Don't worry," Wade said. "We do this kind of thing all the time," he added easily, obviously trying to soothe her nerves. "Approaching people who are skittish while keeping the situation calm and friendly is a major part of our business. We'll smile and do our best not to appear threatening."

Charlotte thought about how she'd be feeling right now if she'd had to make the trip out here by herself. If she hadn't made these new friends. It was hard to believe she'd first met them just two days ago. It was three days ago that she'd met Wade. For so long she'd felt safer on her own and that trusting people would only leave her feeling disappointed and hollow. That the only way to truly feel safe, at least emotionally, was to not rely on anyone else.

She'd learned that from her parents and their obsession with their business.

And now look. Here she was, surrounded by people who took their business seriously but also knew how to keep their personal lives in perspective. She'd prayed for help. The Lord had sent her help. And to receive it, she'd had to trust and rely on other people.

She glanced at Wade's profile, visible in the light from the dashboard. She'd taken a chance relying on him. For physical protection, but even more, for emotional support. And she was glad she had. She'd let him into her heart, although she couldn't say the exact moment when she'd decided to do so, and taking that risk had healed a pretty jaded perspective when it came to her limited expectations from people.

This was an awkward moment for her to wonder how he felt about her, but she couldn't help it. He'd never said he'd changed his initial opinion of her. Not that he'd stated his prejudice toward her so blatantly, but the comments he'd made had expressed his thoughts quite clearly. He'd thought she was spoiled and entitled and clueless about how most people lived simply because of the family she'd been born into.

She hoped he didn't still feel that way about her.

They rounded the final curve in the road.

"There's your sister," Wade said. "She's in the gazebo."

To the left, across the narrow road and opposite the lake, was a fairly large rustic-style home perched midway up a low hill. There was a light on the front porch and one visible through a front window—otherwise, it was dark.

The gazebo was closer to the road. It was a small, white whimsical structure with fairy lights wrapped around the posts, surrounded by a wooden deck, outdoor furniture, a picnic table and a large grill. The perfect setting for outdoor parties in the summer.

Charlotte couldn't help smiling to herself and shaking her head. Of course her sister's quiet retreat had been at a nicely stylish location. An actual cabin, something simple and woodsy, would not have been Dinah's style. Even if her goal had been to sober up, get in touch with her emotions and clear her mind.

Charlotte couldn't see Dinah clearly inside the gazebo, but she could see her sister's shadowy figure as she stood from where she'd been sitting along the railing and looked toward the approaching vehicles with obvious hesitancy.

"Remember, we're going to take everything nice and slow," Wade said as he brought the SUV to a stop. "Things may not be as simple and safe as they look."

It could be a trap.

Charlotte nodded. She'd grown used to the feeling of muscles tightening in her stomach, and here it was again. Like Wade, she scanned their surroundings. The lights spilling from the house, the gazebo lights and the vehicle lights didn't illuminate nearly as much as she would have liked. There was still so much hidden in shadow. Thick trees covered much of the property. To her right, the inky waters of Wolf Lake lapped at the shoreline.

Danny Ryan drove his pickup past them and then made a U-turn before stopping. His headlights crossing with Wade's erased some of the shadows and gave a little clearer view of the expanse of lawn in front of the house and Dinah in the gazebo.

"There's no one in there with her," Wade said to Charlotte. "But that doesn't mean there isn't someone nearby watching. Let us go meet with her first. If everything's good, we'll bring her back here and you can talk all you want on the way back to town."

Wade opened his door. The bounty hunters in the other vehicle followed suit, all of them moving slowly, scanning their surroundings, a hand near the belts at their waists where they could grab pepper spray or a gun if they had to. They were wearing bulletproof vests and had insisted that Charlotte wear one, too.

Dinah appeared vulnerable and uncertain, and she began to back up and look around frantically as Wade and his fellow bounty hunters approached her.

Charlotte rolled down her window, hesitant to wave or call out until she was certain the situation was as safe as it appeared.

As promised, Wade approached Dinah with calm, measured movements. "Dinah Halstead? My name is Wade Fast Horse. I'm a friend of your sister." He managed to sound less like a cop approaching a person of interest and more like an engaging sort of person approaching a mutual friend.

"Where's Charlotte?" Dinah demanded, her voice shaky with uncertainty. She continued to back up until she was almost out of the gazebo. "Why isn't she here? She said she was going to come get me."

"I'm right here!" Charlotte called out through the open window, unable to wait any longer.

Dinah startled and then turned in her direction, squinting at the SUV's headlights and holding her hand up to her forehead as if trying to see past the glare. "Wh-what's going on?"

It took every bit of self-control Charlotte had not to dart out of the car. But nearly getting killed—more than once over the last three days—had taught her the value of keeping control of her emotions in an uncertain situation. "They're my friends and they're just making sure the situation is secure. They want to make sure you don't have someone nearby forcing you to draw me into a trap."

Dinah tilted her head slightly and was quiet for a moment. "How do I know this isn't some weird sort of trap for someone to get at *me*?" she called out. "I can't see you. Maybe somebody is beside you pointing a gun at *you* and making you say things to give me a false sense of security."

Charlotte felt a smile on her lips despite the seriousness of the situation. Her twin might behave like a fool at times, but she was not dumb. And considering that Gamble had meant to target Dinah in the beginning, and a hit man was being paid to come after Charlotte in the meantime, Dinah had a right to be suspicious.

"I think the situation looks secure," Charlotte called out, figuring Wade would know she was talking to him. "I'm going to get out so Dinah can see me."

Wade turned in her direction and gave a tight nod.

The other bounty hunters continued gazing around, keeping an eye on things.

Charlotte opened her door, suddenly feeling a bit nervous about doing it. It would be a relief to collect her sister and get back to the inn. Under different circumstances it would be nice to spend some time out here away from town and near the lake, but right now it felt creepy.

She stepped out onto the gravel drive. A breeze coming off the lake buffeted her hair. The same breeze sent tree branches swaying and creaking.

"Here I am," Charlotte called out. She began to move toward her sister. For the moment she set her frustration with Dinah aside, and let herself focus on the rush of emotions she felt as memories popped into her mind of their childhood when they were so close. It looked like she and Dinah were going to have that chance to rebuild their relationship. *Thank You, Lord.*

Dinah hesitated for a moment, watching her. And then she started moving toward Charlotte.

"You're alive!" Charlotte said when they reached each other and hugged. The emotion of the moment walloped her harder than she'd expected and tears collected in her eyes and then rolled down her cheeks.

"I'm so sorry," Dinah said. "For doing a thoughtless thing like disappearing without telling anyone what I was doing. For not making my loan payments and causing you to get kidnapped when they meant to take me." She started to cry and choke on her words. "For everything."

"Loan payments?" Charlotte asked.

"Yes." Dinah took a step back and wiped at her eyes.

"Things weren't going as well at the coffee shop as they looked. Well, *I* wasn't doing a good job managing it." She looked down for a moment. "In some ways I wasn't managing it at all. I was gone a lot, visiting friends, just because I was bored. And when I got bored I went looking for something to ease that feeling and make the time pass faster."

"You mean you went looking for a drink? Or something else?"

Dinah nodded. "Things got out of control. I started to worry and things got worse. I'd leave more often, figuring I'd just have a quick drink or a smoke and come right back." She shook her head. "Stupid. I was so *stupid*. And embarrassed and I couldn't let Mom and Dad or Ethan know, because I was just so tired of messing things up and I didn't want to face them. Finally, I took out the loan, from a guy one of my friends knew."

"Brett Gamble."

"Yes." Dinah sighed heavily. "When I got the money from him, I told myself I would slowly add it to my deposits for the coffee shop, make my balance sheet look better, make it look like I was doing a good job managing it. And at the same time, I would work harder and smarter. I would get things into shape. I would be able to regain my self-respect."

"But that didn't happen?" Charlotte asked sadly.

Dinah shook her head. "I borrowed a little of the money to take my friends out to dinner and nightclubbing. We had fun and I was able to pay for everything. Because everybody loves a Halstead twin when we pick up the tab, right?"

Charlotte felt her heart break. "There are people who will love you for you," Charlotte said. "I do."

Dinah laughed bitterly and looked away. "Yeah, well, I appreciate that, but I think you overestimate people." She drew herself up. "Anyway, I made some of the payments, but then I missed a few. Brett was fine with that. Said that he would just add it back to what I owed. Before I knew it, I was out of money and I hadn't made payments in a long time. Things at the coffee shop weren't getting any better, either.

"I ignored Brett's calls. People told me he came by the coffee shop looking for me, but of course I wasn't there. So I guess he hired someone to kidnap me, probably to scare me into getting the money to pay him somehow, but the guy grabbed you by mistake.

"I was so used to hiding everything, so used to putting up a false front by then, that I didn't tell you. I didn't tell anyone. I came here for a few days to try to untangle everything in my head."

Charlotte sensed Wade stepping up behind her. A moment later he leaned over her shoulder and said, "Let's get back in the SUV. You and your sister can talk in there." He glanced around. "I don't like standing out here like this. You're too exposed."

They'd found Dinah, but the contract killer was still at large.

Charlotte nodded. "Of course."

Before they started moving, Charlotte asked Dinah, "Why did you move that money from the payroll account into my personal account and make it look like I embezzled funds?" Since her sister seemed desperate to unburden herself with an admission of what she'd been doing, it seemed as good a time as any to ask her. "Were you trying to draw attention away from yourself? Did you intend to eventually move that money into your own account?"

Dinah stopped walking and gave her an odd look. "I didn't move any money into your account. What are you talking about?"

"Look, I know you're embarrassed—"

The sound of gunfire stopped Charlotte midsentence. At the same time, she felt the burning strike of a bullet hitting her body.

"Everybody down!" Wade leaped at Charlotte, knocking her off the steps of the gazebo and then quickly scooting with her until they were hidden behind a pile of large rocks. Shots continued to be fired at them by an unseen shooter hidden in the woods in the direction of Wolf Lake.

From the corner of his eye, Wade caught the quick movement of Hayley as she rushed toward Dinah. Charlotte's twin was already backing up in a panic. Hayley reached her and hurried her out the back of the latticework gazebo, where the two of them were able to hunker down behind a low wall at the edge of the wooden deck.

Connor and Danny likewise took cover, also sprinting beyond and flattening themselves behind the low wall.

Wade's heart thundered in his chest. He'd heard the first shot and seen Charlotte spin halfway around at the same time. He wasn't certain if she'd been struck, but stark fear that she might be critically injured washed over him. He was already shielding her body with his and he leaned even closer, his lips near her ear, in case the assailant was listening to find their location in the silence since the shooting had stopped. "Are you all right?"

"My right arm." Charlotte forced out the words through gritted teeth. She drew in a hissing breath. "I've been shot."

Being careful not to put pressure on her arm as he moved, Wade drew his gun. He had to be prepared in case the attacker came upon them. Then he moved again so he could see how badly she was injured.

It looked to him like she'd been hit twice. It was hard to be certain because of the bulkiness of clothes. There was a fair amount of blood. "Doesn't look too bad," he said, trying to sound less concerned than he felt. "Looks like it did hit your upper arm." He leaned up enough to unfasten and remove his bulletproof vest and then shrug out of his flannel shirt. He wore a black T-shirt underneath. He folded the flannel, laid it over her wound and then set her hand atop it. "Hold that there," he said. "Makes for a bulky bandage, but we have to use what we've got."

"Wade." Connor's voice, quiet and confident, reached him from the other bounty hunters' position behind the gazebo.

"I hear you," Wade answered as he put the vest back on.

"We're okay over here. How about you?"

"Charlotte's been hit."

"But you said it wasn't bad," Charlotte muttered.

"I've got to get her out of here," Wade continued. "I want to get her to the hospital." He wasn't taking any chances.

"I can't get phone reception to call for help." This time it was Hayley's voice. "Can you?"

Wade pulled out his phone. No bars. He tried to call 9-1-1 a couple of times anyway, but it wouldn't go through. "I got nothing."

The shooting hadn't resumed. Maybe the gunman had left.

They couldn't hide here all night. Wade didn't want to stay any longer, not with Charlotte shot and bleeding. He needed to get her into the SUV and drive her into town. "We're going to try to get out of here," he said for Connor and the others to hear.

"Copy that," Connor replied. "Move quickly. We're ready to return fire if the assailant starts shooting again."

"I might not be able to move quickly," Charlotte said beside Wade. "I'm starting to feel a little dizzy."

That was not good.

Lord, please protect all of us.

"Let me make sure the coast is clear before we move. I'm just going to pop my head up for a moment to look around. Hopefully I won't get it shot off."

"Not funny," Charlotte muttered.

Wade leaned down to kiss her on the forehead. It felt like the most natural thing in the world to do. His lips were pressed to her soft skin before he even realized he was going to do it.

At the same time, Charlotte reached up to wrap her hand around his forearm. "Don't you get yourself shot, too, just because you want to show off."

He actually laughed a little. Charlotte's humor given the situation was unexpected. But so much about her was unexpected. Spending time around her, learning who she was under different circumstances, had been frustrating and maddening and charming all at the same time. She'd changed him without meaning to. Just by being herself, being loyal to her problematic sister, by having such backbone. By being a woman a man could trust.

He had to get her to the hospital, get her treated, get her to safety.

He moved slightly away from her, got his feet beneath him so that he was in a squatting position, and slowly rose up so that he could see beyond the boulders they'd been using as a shield.

All was quiet. He stood a little more.

Bang! Bang! Bang!

More shots! But this time coming from the opposite direction of the original gunfire. From an assailant up by the house.

Wade dropped back down.

"Two shooters," Connor called out.

Two shooters had them pinned down. *Now what?*

The shooters could have followed them from the Riverside Inn. At night it was difficult to tell if you were being tailed. Or perhaps they'd already been hidden in place, waiting for Charlotte to arrive so they could launch their attack.

Beside him, Charlotte began to shiver. Wade worried she would go into shock.

"Are we still getting out of here?" she asked.

"I'm not sure if it's wiser to stay or go."

"Why don't you ask me what I think?"

He turned to her and gently ran a fingertip along the side of her face. Her skin was unexpectedly cool and clammy. Not a good sign. "I'm not sure you could make a good judgment call right now."

She locked her gaze on his. "I'm starting to feel really weird. I think I need to get to the hospital."

"Okay. Let's start by seeing if you can walk." Wade took a firm hold on her good arm and helped her get to her feet while they both still remained crouched. Her balance was unsteady.

"You ready to cover us?" Wade asked Connor. He wasn't thrilled to be moving Charlotte under these circumstances, but he had little choice.

"Ready," Connor responded.

Wade offered a quick prayer. And then he called out, "Now!"

Staying as low as they could, Wade and Charlotte moved from behind the rocks and headed for the SUV.

Shots rang out from the direction of the house, the bullets zinging in Wade and Charlotte's direction.

Seconds later, Wade heard return fire from the direction of the gazebo. Meanwhile, he and Charlotte stayed focused on their goal of reaching the SUV. As soon as they reached it, they crouched down and used it as a barricade.

The shooting stopped, and Wade heard Connor shout, "Clear! We got the guy who was shooting from beside the house!"

Rising up slightly to look over the SUV's fender, he saw Connor and Danny with the hit man Paul Boutin. The hired assassin had his hands raised and Danny was cuffing him while Connor stood by, gun in hand but at the moment pointed safely toward the ground.

"They got him," Wade said to Charlotte.

She remained crouched down. In the ambient illumination from the vehicle headlights, he could see that her face was drawn in pain. She looked unsteady and weak and exhausted. Wade's heart fell to his feet.

He needed to get her out of here *now*, before the second shooter started firing again. Hopefully, that assailant had seen Boutin get captured and had decided to run off.

Wade reached to open the SUV door so Charlotte could climb inside.

Bang!

The hidden second attacker shot out a tire. Wade and Charlotte weren't going anywhere.

Danny and Connor rushed into the darkness of the forest to escape the gunfire, pulling their prisoner with them.

Frantic, Wade's mind raced to consider the possible options he and Charlotte had. Maybe they could get to Danny's truck and use that, but they'd have to go out into the open and cross a significant distance to get to it. With the gunman sounding much closer now, that wasn't a reasonable option. Same with attempting to make for the house. Dinah had said it was possible to get reception if you were in the right spot up there, but again, it was too far. He glanced at Charlotte. She looked like she was fading more quickly. At this point maybe the best option would be for her to stay in as safe a spot as possible where she could rest and regain her strength.

They couldn't remain by the SUV. It didn't provide enough protection. "I think we need to go back to where we were," he said to Charlotte. "It'll be safer."

She nodded.

He reached for her hand.

They began to move, and in that same instant he heard an engine start up.

Bright headlights flicked on. The shooter from the lake side of the property must have used the cover of the dark woods to sneak to a vehicle he'd hidden. The engine roared and Wade grasped Charlotte's hand tighter. She obviously moved as quickly as she could, but it wasn't very fast, and she was unsteady on her feet.

The vehicle shot toward them, throwing up gravel behind it, the driver intending to mow them down.

Wade briefly slowed and slid behind Charlotte before speeding up again, half pushing and half carrying her forward. He propelled them around the pile of rocks where they'd hidden before and they both dropped to the ground. He drew his gun, prepared to defend her with every bit of strength he had.

The fast-moving driver slammed on the brakes, but it was too late and the vehicle crashed into the rock pile, the front end becoming stuck. Wade watched as the door flew open and the driver leaped out, hood pulled down low, collar flipped up, face hidden. Gun drawn, he raced toward Wade and Charlotte.

Wade stayed put until just the right moment, leaping up as the driver reached the rock pile and slamming his fist in the man's jaw. The attacker's upper body twisted under the impact, and he flailed his arms as Wade targeted a second punch to the man's gut. He was sent sprawling to the ground, hard.

From the corner of his eye, Wade saw Charlotte slowly stand up. Seeing that she was all right for the moment, he turned his attention back to the unconscious man in front of him. Then he rolled him over so that the assailant was faceup. He pulled up the attacker's hood and yanked down the collar of the jacket so the man's face was visible.

"Ethan," Charlotte said, disbelief making her voice sound hollow. She turned to Hayley, who was now standing and facing in her direction. "That's Dinah's boyfriend."

TWELVE

Charlotte's safety—her *survival*—was all Wade cared about.

Flashing red and blue lights splashed across the gazebo, the trees, and the people talking in clusters or moving about purposefully on the road in front of the elegantly rustic home that had been Dinah's emotional refuge over the last few days.

The scene was relatively calm now. Paramedics continued to treat Charlotte while patrol officers marked the locations of spent bullet casings and any other physical evidence they could find. Detective Romanov spoke with Dinah while the three Ryan siblings gave their points of view regarding all that had happened to the additional detectives who'd arrived with Romanov.

Paul Boutin had already been arrested and driven away.

Ethan Frey had been revived, had refused medical treatment and was seated in the back of a patrol car.

Exactly how Ethan figured into everything remained unclear. So far he'd refused to talk. At the moment, that was the least of Wade's concerns. There would be plenty of time later to put the crime-spree pieces together and to see justice served. Right now, his focus was on Charlotte.

She lay on a gurney in the back of an ambulance with Wade holding her hand. She'd asked if he could be with her, and the paramedic, who happened to be a friend of Wade's, agreed. While the medic monitored her vitals and assessed her wound—she'd been struck by one bullet, not two, as Wade had feared—Wade prayed and thanked God. Everyone had made it through the violent attack and Charlotte's vitals were already improving. It turned out that Charlotte's symptoms, which Wade had feared were signs of blood loss, were actually psychological shock from the terrifying events unfolding around her. Now that the situation was stable and she felt safe, she was recovering from that fairly quickly.

The medic kept up a steady stream of conversation with Charlotte. Probably to assess her mental clarity. So Wade resisted the urge to talk with her for the moment. Instead, he and Charlotte took turns squeezing each other's hands at random moments. And they exchanged glances. Small gestures that gave the bounty hunter the sense of connection with her that he craved.

Wade realized that somehow, at some point, he'd given his heart to Charlotte. Feeling his own physical pain at seeing her in an injured condition confirmed it. It was as if he'd taken his heart from his chest and offered it to her for safekeeping, trusting her to take care of it. His realization that she was truly a trustworthy person had made that possible. The feeling was both terrifying and strengthening at the same time.

In the course of this whole experience with Charlotte, despite all of the terrible events, something inside him had healed. Some part of him that had not wanted to take the emotional risk of falling in love had decided it was worth the chance. And right now he absolutely knew it was worth it. Even with the fear for Charlotte's physical condition that remained over him despite the medic's reassurances.

"It might be a good idea for you to get out of here for a few minutes," the medic said to Wade after asking Charlotte a question and getting no response from her because she was focused on the bounty hunter. "She's stable for right now, but she will need to have the wound taken care of at the hospital. I'll give you a heads-up before we roll out of here."

"I'll be fine," Charlotte said in a slightly creaky voice.

"Of course." Wade gave her hand one more squeeze and then climbed out of the ambulance.

Connor was waiting for him. "How is she?"

"She'll need surgery to repair the injury and X-rays to make certain there are no bullet fragments remaining in the wound. Other than that, she's doing pretty well." Wade was surprised to find his voice choke up a little.

Connor, always the big brother, gave him a strong one-armed hug and slapped him on the back several times.

Wade glanced toward Danny and Hayley, who were still talking to the police. They had both gotten married recently. Wade had been happy for them. Maybe even a little envious, though he would never have admitted to it. Because he'd been convinced that the type of happiness they'd found simply wasn't available to him.

Now? Well, now he was thinking a whole lot differently.

While Connor went to talk to an officer who'd waved him over, Wade headed toward the spot where Detective Romanov was interviewing Dinah. He figured he might as well be useful and see what he could learn and report back to Charlotte. Even when he could force himself to direct his focus toward the criminal case that had played out over the last few days, his mind still wanted to drift back to thoughts of her. He'd never had that problem before.

"How is Charlotte?" Dinah called out as Wade approached. Her arms were crossed over her stomach and she was bent slightly forward. She sounded as nervous as she looked.

Romanov sat with Dinah at the picnic table. In the glow from the fairy lights he could see the detective's stormy facial expression. Having learned from experience, Wade was grateful not to be the object of Romanov's wrath.

It was not a crime for an adult to disappear for a few days without letting anyone know what they were doing. But given everything that had happened, all of it tied back to Dinah, and Wade could understand the detective's frustration. And probably suspicion, too. Maybe Dinah had played everyone. Maybe she had more of a hand in everything than it appeared and that she admitted to.

What if the attacks weren't actually over? Charlotte might continue to be in danger after she was released from the hospital. Maybe even more so, since everyone would have let their guard down.

Anxiety twisted Wade's gut. His mind raced toward thoughts of the embezzled money, of Charlotte being framed and of a hit man being hired to kill Charlotte. Who exactly stood to gain by Charlotte's death? Her twin?

"She's stable," Wade said, realizing he hadn't answered Dinah's question. Right now, he wasn't sure he wanted to tell her much of anything. "Has your boyfriend started talking yet?"

She winced.

Maybe it was a genuine display of emotion and Wade had framed his question a little too harshly. Maybe she truly loved Ethan and had been as shocked as anyone by his behavior. Or maybe she was just a good actress.

Surprisingly, Romanov didn't tell him to go away while she conducted her interview. Instead, she remained quiet and kept her gaze focused on Dinah.

Charlotte and Dinah were identical twins, but now that he knew them, Wade didn't think they looked identical at all. Of course their facial features were similar, but the warmth and compassion and determined good humor he often saw on Charlotte's face was absent from her twin. What he saw in front of him was someone spoiled and self-absorbed and anxious. That was sad. And potentially dangerous.

Dinah shook her head and sighed. "I know it looks bad. I know you think I'm involved with whatever Ethan had planned. But the only thing I did was borrow money from a loan shark and not pay it back." She turned to Romanov. "Like I told you." She returned her gaze to Wade. "Ethan is—*was*—my boyfriend," she corrected. "But obviously I didn't know him as well as I thought I did." She looked down for a moment before lifting her gaze. "I admit I didn't want to be alone and Ethan was, well, he was right there in front of me and I figured he was a stable kind of guy and my parents would approve of him. They've employed him for years. I guess he fooled them, too." Unshed tears collected in the corners of her eyes. "I thought he cared about me, but maybe he was just after the money. I have no idea what his plan was or what he thought he was doing." She shrugged and the tears began to fall. "I don't know what else to say."

Romanov turned to Wade. "Ethan hasn't said a word since he asked for a lawyer."

Dinah offered Wade a weak smile. "Tell Charlotte I wasn't involved with any of this. That I would never hurt her."

"Why don't you tell her yourself? It might make her feel better to hear it directly from you."

She shook her head. "I've burned a lot of bridges with her over the years. She has reason not to believe me. But she'll believe you."

"What makes you so sure of that?"

"Well, she trusted you with her life tonight, didn't she?"

Wade's paramedic buddy called him over to the ambulance. "We're getting ready to transport Charlotte to the hospital," he said as Wade approached. "Before you ask, I don't want you riding in the back with her in case something happens and I need room to move around quickly."

Wade nodded and swallowed thickly, sending up a quick prayer that nothing would happen and that Charlotte's condition would remain stable. Then he popped into the back to tell her he'd be following her to the hospital. "I spoke with Dinah. She says she had nothing to do with the attempts on your life and she knew nothing about them."

Charlotte sighed and smiled widely. "I'm happy to hear that."

Wade just hoped it was really the truth.

He bent over to kiss her forehead. In response, she reached up her hand that wasn't tethered to an IV to brush her fingertips across his cheek.

The shared moment wrapped around him like a warm embrace.

As he backed away, Wade noticed how pale she looked. Fear wriggled to life in his gut. What if the paramedic's assessment was wrong? Anxious to get her to the hospital, he hurried to the SUV and fired up the engine.

The feeling of her touch remained with him, along with the hope it offered that they truly might have a future together. As the ambulance started up the narrow road, he followed behind it, unable to remember when he'd ever felt so happy and so worried both at the same time.

"I guess it's a good sign that they aren't rushing me into surgery…" Charlotte said, her voice trailing off at the end.

Wade couldn't help smiling at the loopy expression on her face. He reached over to brush a few strands of hair from her face.

She wasn't being rushed into surgery, but she was going soon. Meanwhile, now that the adrenaline spike from the attack had subsided, she'd become very aware of the pain from her wound, and the emergency room nurse had given her some medication for that.

They were in a small curtained-off area in the ER with an officer standing guard in the hallway just outside the emergency unit's doors.

After he'd driven away from the crime scene, Romanov had called to let him know she'd be sending an officer to keep an eye on Charlotte until they got everything figured out and they were certain she was no longer in danger.

"Your bail jumpers Brett Gamble and Paul Boutin are both in custody now," she'd added firmly. "That means your job is done. You are not a detective. I know you're concerned for Charlotte, but if you involve yourself in this case going forward, I will arrest you for interfering in a police investigation."

"Understood."

He'd found himself annoyed with his adoptive siblings when he realized that Connor, Danny and Hayley had all jumped into the truck and followed him to the hospital. While he appreciated their support, he'd been hoping for a chance to talk with Charlotte alone. Maybe it was a bad idea, but he wanted to tell her how he felt as soon as possible.

He loved her. He knew it beyond a shadow of a doubt.

He wanted her to know that he realized how foolish he'd been in judging her before he got to know her. And in assuming that because she was a Halstead that she would be self-absorbed and spoiled and shallow. He'd been wrong, and he was surprisingly anxious to admit it.

Maybe it was selfish of him, but he'd wanted to hear that she loved him, too.

He'd managed to ditch his siblings in the lobby, since patients in this section of the hospital were only allowed one visitor at a time.

Now, gazing at the sweet, groggy, loopy expression on Charlotte's face, he realized that he needed to get a hold on his emotions and wait until a better time to tell her how he felt.

He almost laughed aloud as the thought crossed his mind. Having to admonish himself to get a grip on his emotions seemed funny. That was never a problem for him before.

But now? He didn't care if the whole ER staff could hear his declarations and could see how he felt. And given the layout of the place, they probably could.

But Charlotte needed calm and quiet now. And as far as he was concerned, everything was about what she needed. Not what he wanted.

The nurse told him they were about to take her into surgery and asked him to leave.

"I've got to go. They're going to fix you up and I'll see you soon after that."

"Okay." She nodded, sending strands of hair back across her face again.

After giving her a kiss on the cheek and squeezing her hand, Wade left.

He walked past the officer and toward the waiting room, where there seemed to be a crowd of people and something going on.

It turned out the people were there in response to the reports about Charlotte. That she had been shot and her identical twin sister was headed to the Range River police station for questioning.

Over the next hour Wade sat in the waiting area with his bounty hunter family beside him. He watched as Charlotte's parents arrived and reporters and online bloggers photographed them and asked them questions. Well-dressed people who claimed to be good friends of Charlotte's also showed up and they were quick to chat with anyone who would give them a few moments of attention and then post whatever they'd said online.

Wade couldn't help wondering where these *good friends* had been over the last few days when Charlotte could have used their support. Maybe they'd reached out and she'd rebuffed them because she'd been focused on staying alive and finding her sister. Or maybe they weren't interested in getting involved until they could see something in it for them.

She hadn't mentioned friends, much. Wade had gotten the impression that while she had friends on the coast where she'd attended college and built up a church family, she hadn't really had so many that she was truly close to back here in Range River. Maybe the old friends had moved on and she hadn't been back in town long enough to make new ones.

Her parents aside, most of the people who showed up seemed to be there to grab their own piece of online celebrity or catch a little of the glitter from someone else's fame.

He'd almost forgotten that Charlotte had a bit of fame in this town as one of the Halstead twins. And her fame actually went beyond Range River, since the resort had plenty of celebrity visitors and the Halsteads had made a name for themselves in the world of people who could afford to spend money on outdoorsy, north Idaho luxury.

As time passed, and Wade watched and listened to the other people waiting while Charlotte was in surgery, the reality of the gulf between his world and Charlotte's began to sink in.

She was a beautiful young woman from a wealthy family with goals and a future far different from his world of chasing bad guys down dark alleys or tracking them through the woods.

Of course she'd been caught up in the emotion of things. She'd been scared, and as a result she'd understandably been attracted to a man who'd helped to protect her.

Maybe Wade had gotten carried away with emotion, too. Perhaps he'd gotten too caught up in thinking about what she'd given him and hadn't thought enough about whether she wanted anything back. Or whether the connection they'd felt could possibly last once their lives went back to normal.

Perhaps he couldn't have the woman he loved. Maybe he should simply appreciate the blessing that had come as a result of spending time alongside her. Past wounds had healed and he'd found himself able to open his heart much wider than he'd thought possible. He was able to risk believing in someone, something he hadn't been able to bring himself to do in a long time.

A doctor finally came out to speak to Charlotte's parents. Wade hurried over, anxious to know that she was okay. To their credit, Arthur and Kandace Halstead did not send him away.

He learned that everything went well. That Charlotte would be staying overnight, possibly two nights, and that her parents would be allowed to see her soon.

Wade glanced over at the bounty hunters on the sofa, looking exhausted. It was time for all of them to go home. Life had taught him that when harsh reality showed up, it was best to accept it as quickly as possible and move on. And the harsh reality here was that he and Charlotte lived in different worlds. There was simply no option for them to be together as a married couple. He'd been foolish to think otherwise.

"She's in good shape," he said, walking up to the Ryan siblings. "Her parents will want to be with her for as long as she's able to have visitors tonight."

The bounty hunters got to their feet and they all headed for the exit.

Wade would get back to chasing fugitives and let Charlotte return to her normal life, as well. But he'd also be paying close attention to her case, feeling uneasy until Ethan Frey finally told the police everything he knew and Wade was certain that Charlotte was safe.

Detective Romanov had a right to warn Wade from trying to solve the case. Her position was understandable, and he was under no illusions that he could singlehandedly unravel the series of connected attacks, anyway.

But if Charlotte found herself scared or in danger, she *had* to know she could call Wade for help and he would come running.

THIRTEEN

Four days later, Charlotte's rideshare driver pulled up to a storefront office in a modest shopping mall near downtown Range River. Charlotte's doctor had recommended she not drive for at least a couple of weeks.

"We're here," the driver said cheerfully.

Charlotte didn't move. At first she just gazed at the gold lettering on the smoked-glass window: Range River Bail Bonds.

Maybe this was a mistake. Maybe she should have called first. Maybe Wade wasn't even here.

"Oh, let me help you," the driver said before hopping out and opening Charlotte's door for her.

The driver must have noticed her sore arm, with the recent injury being made obvious by the bandaging and the slow, careful way Charlotte moved. Or maybe the friendly woman had seen the news reports in the aftermath of the attack at the lake house and she recognized Charlotte.

There had been plenty of dramatic headlines and malicious bits of gossip and seemingly unending rumors swirling about online for the last four days. Specific facts—other than the reality that the attacks had happened and Dinah had voluntarily vanished for a few days—had remained in short supply. But people hardly seemed to notice. They didn't actually care as much as they'd wanted to be entertained. By somebody else's tragedy. By seeing someone with the aura of money and glamour take a spectacular public fall.

Wade Fast Horse had seemed to care. From the beginning. And Charlotte was about to find out if her impression was true. Maybe, as had been the case for so much of her life, his *caring* was something he'd been paid for. Like the nannies who'd been around when Charlotte and Dinah were growing up. Or the *friendly* employees who'd been friendly because they'd wanted to keep their jobs.

Charlotte got out of the car even though she was a little bit afraid to. Because what if the care and concern Wade had shown wasn't real? What if those warm, light touches and the gentle kisses on her face were impulses of the moment and nothing more? Maybe the man had a brief romance with every damsel in distress that he helped.

You don't really believe that about him. The thought came in an instant.

No, she didn't. But she was afraid, nevertheless.

She'd let herself rely on him and trust him. Something she'd thought she would never be able to do after leaning on people—her parents especially—and having them refuse to help hold her up. Even for a short while. Because they had *important things to do.*

Money to make.

What if now that it wasn't part of his job, Wade didn't want to be someone she could lean on when she needed strength? And what if he wouldn't let her be there for him when he was in need of support? That was something she really, *really* wanted to do. Be the support that someone else needed. Have that kind of close relationship.

The driver shut the car door, gave a cheery wave and drove off.

Charlotte still hesitated.

She'd only managed to drum up the courage to come here because Detective Romanov had given her an excuse. In response to Charlotte's daily inquiry on the status of the ongoing investigation, Romanov had messaged her that there had been a break in the case. But she was in the middle of something, couldn't talk now, and Wade knew the details and he could fill her in.

Not that she was in such a hurry to hear the details. She was afraid of what she might learn about members of her family or other people she knew. Maybe someone close to her had planned it all.

Nevertheless, it provided an excuse for Charlotte to see the bounty hunter again. But she didn't know what to expect. He hadn't called her since she'd last seen him in the hospital emergency room. He hadn't texted her. He hadn't reached out at all.

She remembered seeing Wade in the emergency room, although the details of that were a little fuzzy. Her mother had mentioned that he and three other bounty hunters had stayed in the waiting room until her surgery was over. But after that, nothing.

Nerves fluttered in the pit of her stomach as she took a deep breath and headed for the door, determined to play it cool when she saw him.

She stepped inside, where she saw a reception area with a sofa and padded chairs in the front. Farther back, beyond a low wooden wall with a swinging door, were office desks and visitor chairs.

"Charlotte!" Hayley Ryan called out and smiled broadly.

Connor and Danny, who'd each been sitting at a desk and talking to one another, turned to look at her.

"Hi," Charlotte said, walking toward them as Hayley hurried forward to greet her. Connor and Danny likewise got up to say hello.

Wade remained at a desk, focused on a computer screen while typing in information with a phone pressed to his ear.

"He picked up a new case this morning," Hayley explained to Charlotte.

Charlotte figured her disappointment at his lack of attention toward her must have been written on her face. Well, that was embarrassing.

Hayley walked to Wade and gave his shoulder a light shove. He looked up at her and she gestured toward Charlotte.

As soon as he saw her, she heard him say, "Let me get back to you," and he disconnected the call.

He stood up and took a deep breath.

"I didn't mean to interrupt your work," Charlotte said awkwardly.

"It's all right. I can finish that call later." His gaze shifted from her face to her injured upper arm. "How are you?" His gaze traveled back to her face. "You look good."

"I'm doing well." It took an effort to settle her nerves so her voice wasn't shaky. Now that she was actually here with Wade, she had that feeling again. That sense of being shored up by his presence. Of feeling connected.

Of feeling stupidly giddy and giggly because there was just something about those dark eyes, brown skin with a warm, red undertone and raven hair that made her a little bit light-headed. Especially when he smiled that boyish smile. And he smiled at her right then.

Her response was a grin so wide that her cheeks started to hurt.

So much for playing it cool and not scaring him away.

Not that he was a man who was easily scared away from anything. She knew that from experience.

After they stood and stared at each other for a moment, she finally gathered her thoughts. "I'm glad you weren't out chasing down a bad guy. I guess I should have called first. But Detective Romanov said you could fill me in on the latest details in my case."

Wade raised an eyebrow slightly. "Romanov told you to come see me?"

Charlotte nodded.

He exchanged glances with the Ryans, who were lingering nearby, obviously eavesdropping.

Wade chewed his bottom lip for a moment. "It will take me a few minutes to explain everything. Do you want to grab a coffee from next door? Maybe walk across the street to the park?" He glanced at her arm. "That is, if you feel up to it."

"Sure," Charlotte answered, feeling relieved and keyed up at the same time. "I'd love some coffee. Fresh air is always good."

After a quick round of goodbyes, which included a moment when Danny Ryan smiled widely at his best friend and Wade gave him a menacing look in return, they stepped outside.

Wade held the door for Charlotte as she exited the coffee shop carrying a huge espresso drink, and then he followed her out. "You sure that much caffeine is good for you?" he asked with a nod toward the cup in her hand.

"Oh, I *need* this. Besides, compared to all the surges in adrenaline I've had over the last week as people tried to kill me, the little boost from this drink is nothing."

Wade's laugh in response was partly from her joke and partly from nervous energy. Being away from Charlotte the last four days had been miserable. Instead of getting over her, he'd missed her *more*. And now here she was. Her face more beautiful than he'd remembered. Her smile making him feel like *he* was the one who needed to cut back on caffeine. The sound of her voice soothing and invigorating at the same time.

"How are things with your family?" he asked as they crossed the street. The sky was clear, the sunlight shining down was warm, and the mixture of evergreens and deciduous trees with newly sprouting leaves offered a nice, lacy mixture of light and shadow in the park.

"Things around the resort have been a little tense." Charlotte sat on the top of a picnic table, her feet on the bench seat. Wade stood across from her, wanting to drink in the sight of her. To finally see her fairly relaxed and happy rather than anxious and fearful. Whatever tension she felt at the resort wasn't visible on her face right now.

"Everyone is on pins and needles waiting for the full story to come out," she continued. "The resort tech team finally confirmed that I didn't attempt to embezzle any money. The transactions made to move resort payroll funds into my personal account were done on a work laptop assigned to me. Security video inside the management offices showed Ethan taking my laptop into his office during the time frame when the transactions were made. It's obvious he was trying to set me up and I can only hope that he'll confess to it at some point. Meanwhile, all the money is back where it belongs." She sighed. "My parents have been supportive of Dinah and me after all we've been through, but at the same time, that support is measured." She shrugged. "What else is new? It's always been that way. And Dinah is researching rehab and counseling facilities. Maybe she'll find something that appeals to her and give it a sincere try."

Wade nodded. "I hope so."

"Me, too." She fixed her gaze on him. "I don't know how you deal with potentially life-or-death situations for a living. But I know this has taught me a lot. The most important thing I have is my faith. And I'm leaning into that more than ever now."

"That's the way I get through the dangers and snares of life, too."

She sat up a little straighter. "So, I haven't pressed you to hurry up and tell me the details you've learned about the case because I'm not sure I want to know them." She shrugged. "I guess I'm afraid to learn that Dinah was more criminally involved than she admitted."

"That's not the case. Thanks to a combination of Detective Romanov's excellent interrogation skills and plea bargain offers from the prosecutor, Ethan finally started talking. Gamble and Boutin did, as well. Turns out there were a couple of different things going on at once."

Wade took a deep breath and blew it out. "Dinah was telling the truth. She wasn't doing a good job of managing the coffee shop. She borrowed money from Gamble and stopped making payments. He hired Murphy to grab her and bring her to him so he could scare her into figuring out a way to pay him his money."

"That's when Murphy mistakenly kidnapped me."

"Right. Gamble was just starting out in the loan-sharking business, and he knew if people got away with not paying him back, he was sunk. In his mind, if he didn't get paid, he had to seriously harm or kill someone to maintain a reputation that would keep him in business. That's why he and Murphy were so recklessly willing to shoot at you.

"Once Gamble realized they'd grabbed the wrong person, he figured the police would be keeping a close eye on Dinah. Rather than making a second attempt to grab her, he planned to kidnap you and ransom you back to your parents. That's why they started targeting you."

"Did they hire the hit man?"

"No. Ethan hired him."

Charlotte shook her head. "Why? He seemed so enamored of Dinah. He'd worked for the family for so long. My parents thought so much of him."

"All of that helps to explain why. He hoped to, well, own the resort one day. He figured he'd marry Dinah and eventually inherit half the value of it through her when your parents died. But then he realized Dinah was going off the rails. He knew about her poor management of the coffee shop. Knew she was having substance abuse issues. He was afraid he would become her husband only for your parents to disinherit her and then he would never have his dream come true. Apparently he tried to switch his affections to you and it failed."

"Me?" Charlotte's voice nearly squeaked. "If he tried to make the moves on me, I never even noticed." She shook her head. "I've never been interested in Ethan. Not my type, at all."

"Well, maybe he was insulted by that and it played

into what followed. Dinah disappeared, and apparently he honestly knew nothing about that. He thought she might not be found alive and he got the idea that if both Halstead twins were dead, your grieving parents might look to him as the son they never had and he might actually inherit the resort after all. So he hired the hit man to kill you and figured if Dinah reappeared he'd either convince her to marry him since she would be sure to inherit, being the only surviving child, or if she wouldn't marry him, he'd just wait a bit and have her killed, too."

There was nothing else to add, so Wade just waited quietly.

"I've thought about walking away from it all," Charlotte finally said in a quiet but strong voice. "I've prayed about it. A lot. I get the feeling that I should keep working at the resort and push my parents to use some of the money to the benefit of other people."

"Does that mean you're still planning to go to California for that internship program in San Diego?" Wade asked. *Please say no.* It was a selfish thought, but he'd had a lifetime of remembering the cold fact that people often left, said they'd return, but never did.

She nodded. "Yeah, I'm going." She gave him a shy smile. "But I'll be coming back."

So this was probably the moment he needed to speak up. "I wish you would stay."

Her blue eyes appeared to pick up a bit of a sparkle at that. "Do you?" she asked in a teasing tone. "Why?"

Feeling emboldened, Wade moved a little closer. "Because I got used to seeing you every day and I liked it." He reached out to rub a finger along the line of her jaw and she leaned into it. Maybe the fears that had crept into his mind in the hospital waiting room about the two of them not being able to build a life together had been baseless. Perhaps he hadn't given her enough credit. Or perhaps he hadn't given the both of them enough credit. Each had proved that they could grow and change and they could face difficult situations. Like coming from different backgrounds and different social worlds.

He moved even closer toward her, while sliding his fingertips down the delicate skin until they were under her chin. "I think you might have gotten used to being around me, too." He smiled. "You didn't have to make the trip here to the office to ask me about your case. You could have called."

"I didn't know if what we'd shared was just a working relationship. I thought maybe with your fugitives captured, everything between us would be over. I wanted to see you for myself and find out." She looked flustered and her cheeks turned a pretty shade of pink.

Wade closed the gap between them, brushing his lips across her cheeks and the side of her neck and then finally kissing her until he felt her sigh and relax in his arms. He felt the seriousness of the trust she was placing in him, and he meant to honor it. "So you think there's room for a bounty hunter in your life?"

"Absolutely, yes." She looked at him with eyes filled with love and a hint of mischief. "I can't wait to spend time with you when there isn't someone trying to kill or kidnap me."

He reached for her hands and gave each of them a kiss. "Charlotte Halstead, you have been nothing but trouble since the moment I met you." He leaned in to press another kiss to her lips. "It's a good thing I love trouble."

In that moment, he knew he loved her enough to accept the risk of her leaving town for several months. During that time, he would hope and pray that she would come back.

EPILOGUE

One year later

"It's okay, Mom. Everything doesn't have to be perfect." Wade looked into the mirror where his gaze connected with his mother, who was standing behind him.

His eyes started to sting a little, and he looked away. The happiness in his heart was so strong and sharp that it almost hurt.

Maribel resumed straightening his suit collar, tugging the back of his coat to make sure it hung correctly and brushing his shoulders. As if dust could have landed there in the three or four minutes since she'd last brushed them.

"Let me do this," Maribel said with a slight sniff. As if she were holding back tears. "I want my big bad bounty hunter son to look good on his wedding day."

Wedding day.

Wade Fast Horse was about to get married and he couldn't quite believe it.

"Mom, do you think you'll ever get married again?" He'd asked her that more times than he could count since he was young, starting when his dad had finally initiated the divorce. Her response had always been a laugh, maybe a head shake and a firm answer along the lines of *Not a chance.*

This time, she simply shrugged.

Wade read that as a *maybe.*

"I guess you never know," she added.

Wade's already overwhelmed heart felt like it could burst. The love he felt for Charlotte just kept growing. His bride-to-be had given him courage enough to dare to hope again, and seeing that must have inspired his mom.

What women he had in his life. What a blessed man he was.

Shortly after Wade and Charlotte had become a couple, Charlotte had left for California.

And then she'd come back. Just like she'd promised.

Wade had been anxious while she was gone. Of course, they had talked on the phone and texted. Still, he'd been irritable. So moody that he could hardly stand himself during the long days when he wondered what she was doing. But at the same time he had prayed, had healed and had remembered that the true source of his strength would never leave him nor forsake him. Based on that promise from the Lord, he could take the risk of loving Charlotte.

And, man, was he ever glad he had.

"Hey, do you think you look pretty enough yet?" Danny Ryan knocked lightly on the partially open door and walked in.

"Dude, I will always be prettier than you," Wade joked with his best man. "Try not to be jealous."

They were in the bedroom Wade typically used at the Riverside Inn. The wedding ceremony would be taking place outside, under a white pavilion decorated with flowers and with the river—made sparkly by the bright midday sun—flowing along in the background.

Charlotte had said she wanted a ceremony that was simple and heartfelt. Wade was determined that she would get what she wanted, and Connor had been more than happy to help out by offering the use of the grounds at the inn.

There was another light knock on the door. "Are you dressed?" Hayley called out.

"You can come in," Maribel answered.

Hayley walked into the room with Connor right behind her. "It's time," she said.

Surrounded by his mom and the family that was truly as much his family as the one he had been born into, Wade headed out of the room and downstairs.

A couple of Connor's dogs joined them, both animals wagging their tails and trotting happily as if they understood that this was a very special occasion.

Outside, Wade stopped for a moment to take in the beautiful view in front of him. The flowers and decorations. Nature, stunningly displayed by the view of the river and the forest and mountains in the distance. Friends and family here to help Charlotte and him celebrate their marriage.

He and Danny took their positions in front of the assembled guests, exchanging nods with the pastor.

The music started up, and moments later, Charlotte appeared. She wore a lacy ivory-colored dress with a veil and carried a bouquet of pink and yellow roses.

Her beauty as she approached him took his breath away.

For so long, he wouldn't have even been able to imagine a moment like this.

God truly was the God of the impossible.

And Wade was so very grateful.

The kiss Wade gave Charlotte to mark the end of the ceremony was a little more enthusiastic than she'd anticipated.

Not that she was complaining.

But it was a good thing her brand-new husband was strong enough to hold her up. Because her knees went weak. And for a moment, it felt like every bone in her body had melted.

Of course, their guests laughed and hooted and hollered. The Ryans, most notably. Wade's family. Now *her* family, too.

And this would be her new home. Connor had invited Charlotte and Wade to move in and reside there. Apparently the self-possessed owner of Range River Bail Bonds had decided he liked having a little company on a regular basis. Lots of things were changing, and that was good.

As she and Wade started back down the aisle together, she glanced over at her parents. They looked slightly more relaxed than normal. That was something. And Dinah was looking well, too. She had shown an interest in faith and Charlotte was encouraged by that.

The happy couple made a beeline for the cake, where they served each other first bites, and then got busy serving guests. Because they felt like they had already been given so much. They worked as a team, chatting with guests as they served the cake and doing their best to make everyone feel valued and included.

During their many, many long talks while they were getting to know each other better, Charlotte and Wade had discovered that those were two feelings they'd both always wanted. Feeling valued and included. Now that they had each other, as a married couple they wanted to extend those feelings, and true support, to others.

Faith and love could do so much. They'd both learned that. And they were looking forward to spending the rest of their lives together, sharing that lesson with others.

* * * * *

If you enjoyed this Range River Bounty Hunters story by Jenna Night, pick up these previous books in the series:

Abduction in the Dark
Fugitive Ambush

Available now from Love Inspired Suspense!

Dear Reader,

Thank you for coming along on yet another race to capture the bad guys!

Family stories are interesting to me because no family is perfect, no matter how things look from the outside. Good thing we don't have to be perfect to be lovable.

I'm gearing up to write the story of the final member of the Ryan family, the owner and founder of Range River Bail Bonds, Connor Ryan. This man has some secrets that are about to be exposed. I hope he's ready!

I invite you to visit my website, jennanight.com. You can also keep up with me on my Jenna Night Facebook page or get alerts about upcoming books by following me on BookBub. My email address is Jenna@JennaNight.com. I'd love to hear from you.

Jenna Night

ALASKAN AVALANCHE ESCAPE
K-9 Search and Rescue • by Darlene L. Turner

After discovering someone is deliberately triggering avalanches, mountain survival expert Jayla Hoyt and her K-9 set out to stop the culprit—but he sets his sights on them. Can she and Alaska park ranger Bryson Clarke catch the criminal before they all lose their lives?

GUARDING HIS CHILD
by Karen Kirst

Following her best friend's gruesome murder, Deputy Skye Saddler is assigned to protect the victim's baby and the father who didn't know the little girl existed. Now that rancher Nash Wilder is the killer's next target, keeping close to Skye is their best chance at survival.

DETECTING SECRETS
Deputies of Anderson County • by Sami A. Abrams

When pregnant teens and babies go missing, Sheriff Dennis Monroe works with marriage and family therapist Charlotte Bradley and her air-scent dog to put an end to a black-market baby smuggling ring in Anderson County. But when the kidnapper's scheme includes Charlotte, can she rely on Dennis to protect her?

PERILOUS SECURITY DETAIL
Honor Protection Specialists • by Elizabeth Goddard

When bodyguard Everly Honor rescues her secretive ex-boyfriend from an intentional hit-and-run, he hires her to guard his niece. But with danger closing in on all sides, Sawyer Blackwood must reveal hidden truths...or put their lives at risk.

DEADLY VENGEANCE
by Jodie Bailey

Someone wants profiler Gabe Buchanan dead, and he has no idea why. When his identity is wiped clean, he's forced to trust military investigator Hannah Austin, the woman who hurt him in the past, to restore his life. As deadly threats escalate, they'll have to find the culprit before it's too late.

THEME PARK ABDUCTION
by Patsy Conway

A cartel kidnaps Rebecca Salmon's son off a roller coaster, and now she needs help from FBI agent Jake Foster to solve a series of clues planted throughout the theme park. As they race against time and evade henchmen gunning for them, will Jake's secrets get in the way of saving her son?

———

Get 4 FREE REWARDS!

We'll send you 2 FREE Books plus 2 FREE Mystery Gifts.

FREE
Value Over
$20

Both the **Love Inspired®** and **Love Inspired® Suspense** series feature compelling novels filled with inspirational romance, faith, forgiveness and hope.